Taste
and Other Tales

ROALD DAHL

Level 5

Selected and retold by Michael Caldon
Series Editors: Andy Hopkins and Jocelyn Potter

Contents

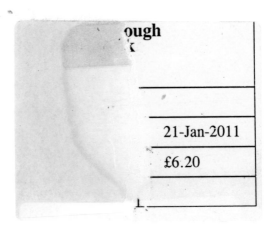

ough

21-Jan-2011

£6.20

Introduction

As we sat down, I remembered that on both Richard Pratt's last visits Mike had played a little betting game with him over the claret. He had asked him to name it and guess its age.

Two men – friends, of course – playing a little game over their meal. What could be more pleasant?

But the author of the short story 'Taste' is Roald Dahl. Things are not what they seem. Dahl's readers soon realize that his stories and the characters in them are rarely pleasant. The little games that they play often become nasty. Richard Pratt, the epicure, is an evil and cruel man who cannot bear to be wrong. It is not long before his unpleasant behaviour involves not only his host, Mike Schofield, but Mike's wife and daughter too.

Roald Dahl made himself a master of a difficult form of literature, the short story. There is no time to develop a character in a short story – we understand what a character is from what he does. A good short story often leaves the reader with a slight shock or a sudden surprise, often called 'the twist in the tail'. Dahl's stories are like this and he quickly became one of the most popular and widely read writers of the twentieth century.

Dahl wrote more than sixty short stories. He first gained success with them in 1953 with *Someone Like You* and his last book, *Collected Stories*, appeared in 2006.

Many of Dahl's stories have become more widely known through films for television and cinema, but people still enjoy reading them too. Readers are entertained and sometimes alarmed by the way ordinary men and women – like Mr Botibol in 'A Swim' or Mary Maloney in 'The Leg of Lamb' – take an idea to extremes or make a sudden decision that changes their lives. The strange behaviour of Dahl's characters causes unexpected events that make the reader feel less comfortable than before.

For nearly twenty years Dahl wrote short stories for adults, and there was a novel too – *My Uncle Oswald* (1979). His first full-length book, *The Gremlins* (1943), though, was written for children. Later, his books for children brought him further recognition and success in England and the United States. The best-known are: *James and the Giant Peach* (1961), *Charlie and the Chocolate Factory* (1964), *The BFG* (1982) and *Matilda* (1988).

Dahl's stories for children are often as strange and shocking as his stories for adults. Children fight against unfeeling relatives and cruel teachers, usually with a good deal of success. They often succeed in embarrassing the adults who so often hurt the children in their care.

Children love Dahl's books because of the lively conversation and unusual plots. The author has a way with words that they find very amusing. One of his most popular characters, the BFG (Big Friendly Giant), makes up strange-sounding words and uses them in his odd conversations. Children enjoy this word–play and have no difficulty in understanding it.

Children, like their parents, also enjoy the excitement of the unexpected. They can perhaps accept it more easily. They know that, although the powerful and strong enjoy threatening the weak, sometimes the weak can win if they are brave enough.

All writers are affected by their backgrounds and early experiences. Roald Dahl was no exception. He was born in South Wales in 1916, in the middle of the First World War. Both his parents were Norwegian, and as a child Roald spoke Norwegian at home, not English. There was much sadness in his early life. Roald's father died when his son was three, just a month after the death of one of Roald's sisters, Astri.

Roald was sent away from home to be educated at English schools, as his father had wished, but his school days were very unhappy. Roald and his friends were often cruelly punished, and he never forgot the unkindnesses of his teachers. He was popular, though, with the other pupils and he was good at sports. His school holidays were spent sailing and walking in Norway.

Roald Dahl worked for the petrol company Shell when he left school, and when the Second World War started he was in Africa. In November 1939, he joined the British air force. He became a pilot and had many adventures before he was forced to leave flying duties as a result of war wounds. Dahl then went to Washington, where he worked for British interests but also wrote a report based on his own experiences called 'Shot Down over Libya'.

In 1953, Dahl married the actress and film star Patricia Neal, and the couple had five children. After several family tragedies, the marriage ended in 1983, and later Dahl married for the second time. By 1960, he was living in England and was a popular author whose books came out on both sides of the Atlantic. Several of his children's books were made into highly successful films. Roald Dahl died in 1990, but his stories still enjoy great popularity with both adults and children.

Adults continue to be excited by his dark imagination, and children read his tales with as much enthusiasm as their parents did. Roald Dahl was a very rich man when he died. His money was used to form an organization which helps sick people, encourages reading and also helps children enjoy music. There is a Roald Dahl Museum and Story Centre for visitors of all ages, and readers in other countries can find out more about his work – and have fun – on the Internet at www.roalddahl.com. Good bookshops always have his books on their shelves.

Taste

There were six of us at dinner that night at Mike Schofield's house in London: Mike and his wife and daughter, my wife and I, and a man called Richard Pratt.

Richard Pratt was famous for his love of food and wine. He was president of a small society known as the Epicures, and each month he sent privately to its members information about food and wines. He organized dinners where wonderful dishes and rare wines were served. He refused to smoke for fear of harming his ability to taste, and when discussing a wine, he had a strange habit of describing it as if it were a living being. 'A sensible wine,' he would say, 'rather shy but quite sensible.' Or, 'A good-humoured wine, kind and cheerful – slightly rude perhaps, but still good-natured.'

I had been to dinner at Mike's twice before when Richard Pratt was there, and on each occasion Mike and his wife had cooked a very special meal for the famous epicure. And this one, clearly, was to be no exception. The yellow roses on the dining table, the quantity of shining silver, the three wine glasses to each person and, above all, the faint smell of roasting meat from the kitchen brought on a strong desire for the immediate satisfaction of my hunger.

As we sat down, I remembered that on both Richard Pratt's last visits Mike had played a little betting game with him over the claret. He had asked him to name it and to guess its age. Pratt had replied that that should not be too difficult if it was one of the great years. Mike had then bet him a case of that same wine that he could not do it. Pratt had accepted, and had won both times. Tonight I felt sure that the little game would be played again, since Mike was quite ready to lose the bet to prove that his wine was good enough to be recognized, and Pratt seemed to take pleasure in showing his knowledge.

⁕ The meal began with a plate of fish, fried in butter, and to go with it there was a Mosel wine. Mike got up and poured the wine himself, and when he sat down again, I could see that he was watching Richard Pratt. He had set the bottle in front of me so that I could read its name. It said, 'Geierslay Ohligsberg 1945'. He leaned over and whispered to me that Geierslay was a small village in the Mosel area, almost unknown outside Germany. He said that this wine we were drinking was something unusual, and that so little of this wine was produced that it was almost impossible for a stranger to get any of it. He had visited Geierslay personally the summer before in order to obtain the few bottles that they had allowed him to have.

'I doubt whether anyone else in the country has any of it at the moment,' he said.

I saw him look again at Richard Pratt. 'The great thing about Mosel,' he continued, raising his voice, 'is that it's the perfect wine to serve before a claret. A lot of people serve a Rhine wine instead, but that's because they don't know any better.'

Mike Schofield was a man who had become very rich very quickly and now also wanted to be considered someone who understood and enjoyed the good things in life.

'An attractive little wine, don't you think?' he added. He was still watching Richard Pratt. I could see him give a quick look down the table each time he dropped his head to take a mouthful of fish. I could almost feel him waiting for the moment when Pratt would drink his first drop, and look up from his glass with a smile of pleasure, perhaps even of surprise, and then there would be a discussion and Mike would tell him about the village of Geierslay.

But Richard Pratt did not taste his wine. He was too deep in conversation with Mike's eighteen-year-old daughter, Louise. He

2

was half turned towards her, smiling at her, telling her, as far as I could hear, some story about a cook in a Paris restaurant. As he spoke, he leaned closer and closer to her, and the poor girl leaned as far as she could away from him, smiling politely and looking not at his face but at the top button of his dinner jacket.

We finished our fish, and the servant came round and took away the plates. When she came to Pratt, she saw that he had not yet touched his food, so she waited, and Pratt noticed her. He quickly began to eat, pushing the pieces of fish into his mouth with rapid movements of his fork. Then, when he had finished, he reached for his glass, and in two short swallows he poured the wine down his throat and turned immediately to continue his conversation with Louise Schofield.

Mike saw it all. I was conscious of him sitting there, very still, looking at his guest. His round, cheerful face seemed to loosen slightly, but he controlled himself and said nothing.

Soon the servant came forward with the second course. This was a large joint of roast meat. She placed it on the table in front of Mike, who stood up and cut it very thinly, laying the pieces gently on the plates for her to take to the guests. When everyone had been served, he put down the knife and leaned forward with both hands on the edge of the table.

'Now,' he said, speaking to all of us but looking at Richard Pratt. 'Now for the claret. I must go and get it, if you'll excuse me.'

'Get it?' I said. 'Where is it?'

'In my study, already open; it's breathing.'

'Why the study?'

'It's the best place in the house for a wine to reach room temperature. Richard helped me to choose it last time he was here.'

At the sound of his name, Richard looked round.

'That's right, isn't it?' Mike said.

'Yes,' Pratt answered seriously. 'That's right.'

3

'On top of the green cupboard in my study,' Mike said. 'That's the place we chose. A good spot in a room with an even temperature. Excuse me now, will you, while I get it.'

The thought of another wine to play with had cheered him up, and he hurried out of the door. He returned a minute later more slowly, walking softly, holding in both hands a wine basket in which a dark bottle lay with the name out of sight, facing downwards. 'Now!' he cried as he came towards the table. 'What about this one, Richard? You'll never name this one!'

Richard Pratt turned slowly and looked up at Mike, then his eyes travelled down to the bottle in its small basket. He stuck out his wet lower lip, suddenly proud and ugly.

'You'll never get it,' Mike said. 'Not in a hundred years.'

'A claret?' Richard Pratt said, rather rudely.

'Of course.'

'I suppose, then, that not much of this particular claret is produced?'

'Perhaps it is, Richard. And perhaps it isn't.'

'But it's a good year? One of the great years?'

'Yes, I can promise that.'

'Then it shouldn't be too difficult,' Richard Pratt said, speaking slowly, looking extremely bored. But to me there was something strange about his way of speaking; between the eyes there was a shadow of something evil, and this gave me a faint sense of discomfort as I watched him.

'This one is really rather difficult,' Mike said. 'I won't force you to bet on this one.'

'Really. And why not?'

'Because it's difficult.'

'That's rather an insult to me, you know.'

'My dear man,' Mike said, 'I'll have a bet on it with pleasure, if that's what you wish.'

'It shouldn't be too hard to name it.'

4

'You mean you want to bet?'

'I'm perfectly ready to bet,' Richard Pratt said.

'All right, then, we'll bet the usual. A case of the wine itself.'

'You don't think I'll be able to name it, do you?'

'As a matter of fact, and with respect, I don't,' Mike said. He was trying to remain polite, but Pratt was making little attempt to hide his low opinion of the whole business. Strangely, though, his next question seemed to show a certain interest.

'Would you like to increase the bet?'

'No, Richard. A case is enough.'

'Would you like to bet fifty cases?'

'That would be silly.'

Mike stood very still behind his chair at the head of the table, carefully holding the bottle in its basket. There was a whiteness about his nose now and his mouth was shut very tightly.

Pratt was sitting back in his chair, looking up at Mike. His eyes were half closed, and a little smile touched the corners of his lips. And again I saw, or thought I saw, something very evil about the man's face.

'So you don't want to increase the bet?'

'As far as I'm concerned, I don't care,' Mike said. 'I'll bet you anything you like.'

The three women and I sat quietly, watching the two men. Mike's wife was becoming annoyed; I felt that at any moment she was going to interrupt. Our meat lay in front of us on our plates, slowly steaming.

'So you'll bet me anything I like?'

'That's what I told you. I'll bet you anything you like.'

'Even ten thousand pounds?'

'Certainly I will, if that's the way you want it.' Mike was more confident now. He knew quite well that he could afford any sum that Pratt mentioned.

'So you say that I can name the bet?' Pratt asked again.

5

'That's what I said.'

There was a pause while Pratt looked slowly round the table, first at me, then at the three women, each in turn. He seemed to be reminding us that we were witnesses to the offer.

'Mike!' Mrs Schofield said. 'Mike, why don't we stop this nonsense and eat our food. It's getting cold.'

'But it isn't nonsense,' Pratt told her calmly. 'We're making a little bet.'

I noticed the servant standing at the back of the room, holding a dish of vegetables, wondering whether to come forward with them or not.

'All right, then,' Pratt said. 'I'll tell you what I want you to bet.'

'Tell me then,' Mike said. 'I don't care what it is. I'll bet.'

Again the little smile moved the corners of Pratt's lips, and then, quite slowly, looking at Mike all the time, he said, 'I want you to bet me the hand of your daughter in marriage.'

Louise Schofield gave a jump. 'Hey!' she cried. 'No! That's not funny! Look here, Daddy, that's not funny at all.'

'No, dear,' her mother said. 'They're only joking.'

'I'm not joking,' Richard Pratt said.

'It's stupid,' Mike said. Once again, he was not in control of the situation.

'You said you'd bet anything I liked.'

'I meant money.'

'You didn't *say* money.'

'That's what I meant.'

'Then it's a pity you didn't say it. But, if you wish to take back your offer, that's quite all right with me.'

'It's not a question of taking back my offer, old man. It's not a proper bet because you haven't got a daughter to offer me in case you lose. And if you had, I wouldn't want to marry her.'

'I'm glad of that, dear,' his wife said.

'I'll offer anything you like,' Pratt announced. 'My house, for example. How about my house?'

'Which one?' Mike asked, joking now.

'The country one.'

'Why not the other one as well?'

'All right, then, if you wish it. Both my houses.'

At that point I saw Mike pause. He took a step forward and placed the bottle in its basket gently down on the table. His daughter too had seen him pause.

'Now, Daddy!' she cried. 'Don't be *stupid*! It's all too silly for words. I refuse to be betted on like this.'

'Quite right, dear,' her mother said. 'Stop it immediately, Mike, and sit down and eat your food.'

Mike ignored her. He looked over at his daughter and he smiled, a slow, fatherly, protective smile. But in his eyes, suddenly, shone the faint light of victory. 'You know,' he said, smiling as he spoke, 'you know, Louise, we ought to think about this a bit.'

'Now stop it, Daddy! I refuse even to listen to you! Why, I've never heard anything so crazy in all my life!'

'No, seriously, my dear. Just wait a moment and hear what I have to say.'

'But I don't *want* to hear it.'

'Louise, please! It's like this. Richard, here, has offered us a serious bet. He is the one who wants to make it, not me. And if he loses, he will have to hand over a large amount of property. Now wait a minute, my dear, don't interrupt. The point is this. *He cannot possibly win.*'

'He seems to think he can.'

'Now listen to me, because I know what I'm talking about. The claret I've got here comes from a very small wine-growing area that is surrounded by many other small areas that produce different varieties of wine. He'll never get it. It's impossible.'

'You can't be sure of that,' his daughter said.

'I'm telling you I can. Though I say it myself, I understand

7

quite a bit about this wine business, you know. Heavens, girl, I'm your father and you don't think I'd make you do – do something you didn't want to do, do you? I'm trying to make you some money.'

'Mike!' his wife said sharply. 'Stop it now, Mike, please!'

Again, he ignored her. 'If you will take this bet,' he said to his daughter, 'in ten minutes you'll be the owner of two large houses.'

'But I don't want two large houses, Daddy.'

'Then sell them. Sell them back to him immediately. I'll arrange all that for you. And then, just think of it, my dear, you'll be rich! You'll be independent for the rest of your life!'

'Oh, Daddy, I don't like it. I think it's silly.'

'So do I,' the mother said. 'You ought to be ashamed of yourself, Michael, for even suggesting such a thing! Your own daughter too!'

Mike did not look at her. 'Take it!' he said eagerly, looking hard at the girl. 'Take it, quickly! I promise you won't lose.'

'But I don't like it, Daddy.'

'Come on, girl. Take it!'

Mike was pushing her hard. He was leaning towards her, and fixing her with two bright, determined eyes, and it was not easy for his daughter to refuse him.

'But what if I lose?'

'I keep telling you, you can't lose.'

'Oh, Daddy, must I?'

'I'm making you a fortune. So come on now. What do you say, Louise? All right?'

For the last time, she paused. Then she gave a helpless little movement of the shoulders and said, 'Oh, all right, then. Just so long as you swear there's no danger of losing.'

'Good!' Mike cried. 'That's fine! Then it's a bet!'

'Yes,' Richard Pratt said, looking at the girl. 'It's a bet.'

Immediately, Mike picked up the wine and walked excitedly

round the table, filling up everybody's glasses. Now everybody was watching Richard Pratt, watching his face as he reached slowly for his glass with his right hand and lifted it to his nose. The man was about fifty years old and he did not have a pleasant face. Somehow, it was all mouth – mouth and lips – the full, wet lips of the professional epicure. The lower lip hung down in the centre, a permanently open taster's lip. Like a keyhole, I thought, watching it; his mouth is like a large wet keyhole.

Slowly he lifted the glass to his nose. The point of his nose entered the glass and moved over the surface of the wine. He moved the wine gently around in the glass to smell it better. He closed his eyes, and now the whole top half of his body, the head and neck and chest, seemed to become a kind of large sensitive smelling-machine.

Mike, I noticed, was sitting back in his chair, trying to appear unconcerned, but he was watching every movement. Mrs Schofield, the wife, sat upright at the other end of the table, looking straight ahead, her face tight with disapproval. The daughter, Louise, had moved her chair away a little and sideways, facing the epicure, and she, like her father, was watching closely.

For at least a minute, the smelling process continued; then, without opening his eyes or moving his head, Pratt lowered the glass to his mouth and poured in almost half the wine. He paused, his mouth full, getting the first taste. And now, without swallowing, he took in through his lips a thin breath of air which mixed with the wine in the mouth and passed on down into his lungs. He held his breath, blew it out through his nose, and finally began to roll the wine around under his tongue.

It was an impressive performance.

'Um,' he said, putting down the glass, moving a pink tongue over his lips. 'Um – yes. A very interesting little wine – gentle and graceful. We can start by saying what it is *not*. You will pardon me for doing this carefully, but there is much to lose. Usually I would

9

perhaps take a bit of a chance, but this time I must move carefully, must I not?' He looked up at Mike and he smiled, a thick-lipped, wet-lipped smile. Mike did not smile back.

'First, then, which area of Bordeaux does this wine come from? That's not too difficult to guess. It's far too light to be from either St Emilion or Graves. It's obviously a Médoc. There's no doubt about *that*. Now, from which part of Médoc does it come? That should not be too difficult to decide. Margaux? No, it cannot be Margaux. Pauillac? It cannot be Pauillac, either. It is too gentle for Pauillac. No, no, this is a very gentle wine. Unmistakably this is a St Julien.'

He leaned back in his chair and placed his fingers carefully together. I found myself waiting rather anxiously for him to go on. The girl, Louise, was lighting a cigarette. Pratt heard the match strike and he turned on her, suddenly very angry. 'Please!' he said. 'Please don't do that! It's a terrible habit, to smoke at table!'

She looked up at him, slowly and disrespectfully, still holding the burning match in one hand. She blew out the match, but continued to hold the unlighted cigarette in her fingers.

'I'm sorry, my dear,' Pratt said, 'but I simply cannot have smoking at table.'

She didn't look at him again.

'Now, let me see – where were we?' he said. 'Ah yes. This wine is from Bordeaux, from St Julien, in the area of Médoc. So far, so good. But now we come to the more difficult part – the name of the producer. For in St Julien there are so many, and as our host so rightly remarked, there is often not much difference between the wine of one and the wine of another. But we shall see.'

He picked up his glass and took another small drink.

'Yes,' he said, sucking his lips, 'I was right. Now I am sure of it. It's from a very good year – from a great year, in fact. That's better! Now we are closing in! Who are the wine producers in the area of St Julien?'

Again he paused. He took up his glass. Then I saw his tongue shoot out, pink and narrow, the end of it reaching into the wine. A horrible sight. When he lowered his glass, his eyes remained closed. Only his lips were moving, sliding over each other like two pieces of wet rubber.

'There it is again!' he cried. 'Something in the middle taste. Yes, yes, of course! Now I have it! The wine comes from around Beychevelle. I remember now. The Beychevelle area, and the river and the little port. Could it actually be Beychevelle itself? No, I don't think so. Not quite. But it is somewhere very close. Talbot? Could it be Talbot? Yes, it could. Wait one moment.'

He drank a little more wine, and out of the corner of my eye I noticed Mike Schofield and how he was leaning further and further forward over the table, his mouth slightly open, his small eyes fixed on Richard Pratt.

'No, I was wrong. It is not a Talbot. A Talbot comes forward to you just a little more quickly than this one; the fruit is nearer the surface. If it is a '34, which I believe it is, then it couldn't be a Talbot. Well, well, let me think. It is not a Beychevelle and it is not a Talbot, but – but it is so close to both of them, so close, that it must be from somewhere almost in between. Now, which could that be?'

He was silent, and we waited, watching his face. Everyone, even Mike's wife, was watching him now. I heard the servant put down the dish of vegetables on a table behind me, gently, so as not to break the silence.

'Ah!' he cried. 'I have it! Yes, I think I have it!'

For the last time, he drank some wine. Then, still holding the glass up near his mouth, he turned to Mike and he smiled, a slow, silky smile, and he said, 'You know what this is? This is the little Château Branaire-Ducru.'

Mike sat tight, not moving.

'And the year, 1934.'

11

We all looked at Mike, waiting for him to turn the bottle around in its basket.

'Is that your final answer?' Mike said.

'Yes, I think so.'

'Well, is it, or isn't it?'

'Yes, it is.'

'What was the name again?'

'Château Branaire-Ducru. Pretty little farm. Lovely old house. I know it quite well. I can't think why I didn't recognize it immediately.'

'Come on, Daddy,' the girl said. 'Turn the bottle round and let's have a look. I want my two houses.'

'Just a minute,' Mike said. 'Wait just a minute.' He was sitting very quiet, and his face was becoming pale, as though all the force was flowing slowly out of him.

'Michael!' his wife called out sharply from the other end of the table. 'What's the matter?'

'Keep out of this, Margaret, will you please.'

Richard Pratt was looking at Mike, smiling with his mouth, his eyes small and bright. Mike was not looking at anyone.

'Daddy!' the daughter cried. 'You don't mean to say he guessed it right!'

'Now, stop worrying, my dear,' Mike said. 'There's nothing to worry about.'

I think it was more to get away from his family than anything else that Mike then turned to Richard Pratt and said, 'I think you and I had better go into the next room and have a little talk.'

'I don't want a little talk,' Pratt said. 'All I want is to see the name on that bottle.'

He knew he was a winner now and I could see that he was prepared to become thoroughly nasty if there was any trouble. 'What are you waiting for?' he said to Mike. 'Go on and turn it round.'

12

Then this happened: the servant, a small, upright figure in her white-and-black uniform, was standing beside Richard Pratt, holding something out in her hand. 'I believe these are yours, sir,' she said.

Pratt looked round, saw the pair of glasses that she held out to him, and for a moment he paused. 'Are they? Perhaps they are, I don't know.'

'Yes, sir, they're yours.' The servant was an old woman – nearer seventy than sixty – a trusted employee of the family for many years. She put the glasses down on the table beside him.

Without thanking her, Pratt picked them up and slipped them into his top pocket.

But the servant did not go away. She remained standing beside Richard Pratt, and there was something so unusual in her manner and in the way she stood there, small, still and upright, that I found myself watching her with sudden anxiety. Her old grey face had a cold, determined look.

'You left them in Mr Schofield's study,' she said. Her voice was unnaturally, deliberately polite. 'On top of the green cupboard in his study, sir, when you happened to go in there by yourself before dinner.'

It took a few moments for the full meaning of her words to be understood, and in the silence that followed I saw Mike slowly pulling himself up in his chair, and the colour coming to his face, and his eyes opening wide, and the curl of his mouth – and a dangerous whiteness beginning to spread around his nose.

'Now, Michael!' his wife said. 'Keep calm now, Michael, dear! Keep calm!'

A Swim

On the morning of the third day, the sea calmed. Even the most delicate passengers — those who had not been seen around the ship since sailing time — came out of their rooms and made their way slowly onto the sundeck and sat there, with their faces turned to the pale January sun.

It had been fairly rough for the first two days, and this sudden calm, and the sense of comfort that came with it, made the whole ship seem much friendlier. By the time evening came, the passengers, with twelve hours of good weather behind them, were beginning to feel more courageous. At eight o'clock that night, the main dining room was filled with people eating and drinking with the confident appearance of experienced sailors.

The meal was not half over when the passengers realized, by the slight movement of their bodies on the seats of their chairs, that the big ship had actually started rolling again. It was very gentle at first, just a slow, lazy leaning to one side, then to the other, but it was enough to cause a slight but immediate loss of good humour around the room. A few of the passengers looked up from their food, waiting, almost listening for the next roll, smiling nervously, with little secret looks of fear in their eyes. Some were completely calm; others were openly pleased with themselves and made jokes about the food and the weather in order to annoy the few who were beginning to suffer. The movement of the ship then became rapidly more and more violent, and only five or six minutes after the first roll had been noticed, the ship was swinging heavily from side to side.

At last, a really bad roll came, and Mr William Botibol, sitting at the purser's table, saw his plate of fish sliding suddenly away from under his fork. Everybody, now, was reaching for plates and wine glasses. Mrs Renshaw, seated at the purser's right, gave a little scream and held onto that gentleman's arm.

'It's going to be a rough night,' the purser said, looking at Mrs Renshaw. 'I think there's a storm coming that will give us a very rough night.' There was just the faintest suggestion of pleasure in the way he said it.

Most of the passengers continued with their meal. A small number, including Mrs Renshaw, got carefully to their feet and made their way between the tables and through the doorway, trying to hide the urgency they felt.

'Well,' the purser said, 'there she goes.' He looked round with approval at the remaining passengers who were sitting quietly, with their faces showing openly that pride that travellers seem to take in being recognized as 'good sailors'.

When the eating was finished and the coffee had been served, Mr Botibol, who had been unusually serious and thoughtful since the rolling started, suddenly stood up and carried his cup of coffee around to Mrs Renshaw's empty place, next to the purser. He seated himself in her chair, then immediately leaned over and began to whisper urgently in the purser's ear. 'Excuse me,' he said, 'but could you tell me something, please?'

The purser, small and fat and red, bent forward to listen. 'What's the trouble, Mr Botibol?'

'What I want to know is this.' The man's face was anxious and the purser was watching it. 'What I want to know is: will the captain already have made his guess at the day's run – you know, for the competition? I mean, will he have done so before it began to get rough like this?'

The purser lowered his voice, as one does when answering a whisperer. 'I should think so – yes.'

'About how long ago do you think he did it?'

'Some time this afternoon. He usually does it in the afternoon.'

'About what time?'

'Oh, I don't know. Around four o'clock I should think.'

'Now tell me another thing. How does the captain decide which number it will be? Does he take a lot of trouble over that?'

The purser looked at the anxious face of Mr Botibol and smiled, knowing quite well what the man was trying to find out. 'Well, you see, the captain has a little meeting with the second officer, and they study the weather and a lot of other things, and then they make their guess.'

Mr Botibol thought about this answer for a moment. Then he said, 'Do you think the captain knew there was bad weather coming today?'

'I couldn't tell you,' the purser replied. He was looking into the small black eyes of the other man, seeing two single little spots of excitement dancing in their centres. 'I really couldn't tell you, Mr Botibol. I wouldn't know.'

'If this gets any worse, it might be worth buying some of the low numbers. What do you think?' The whispering was more urgent, more anxious now.

'Perhaps it will,' the purser said. 'I doubt whether the captain allowed for a really rough night. It was quite calm this afternoon when he made his guess.'

The others at the table had become silent and were trying to hear what the purser was saying.

'Now suppose *you* were allowed to buy a number, which one would *you* choose today?' Mr Botibol asked.

'I don't know what the range is yet,' the purser patiently answered. 'They don't announce the range until the auction starts after dinner. And I'm really not very good at it in any case. I'm only the purser, you know.'

At that point, Mr Botibol stood up. 'Excuse me, everyone,' he said, and he walked carefully away between the other tables. Twice he had to catch hold of the back of a chair to steady himself against the ship's roll.

As he stepped out onto the sundeck, he felt the full force of the wind. He took hold of the rail and held on tight with both hands, and he stood there looking out over the darkening sea where the great waves were rising up high.

'Quite bad out there, isn't it, sir?' said a waiter, as he went back inside again.

Mr Botibol was combing his hair back into place with a small red comb. 'Do you think we've slowed down at all because of the weather?' he asked.

'Oh, yes, sir. We've slowed down a great deal since this started. You have to slow down in weather like this or you'll be throwing the passengers all over the ship.'

Down in the smoking room people were already arriving for the auction. They were grouping themselves politely around the various tables, the men a little stiff in their dinner jackets, a little pink beside their cool, white-armed women. Mr Botibol took a chair close to the auctioneer's table. He crossed his legs, folded his arms, and settled himself in his seat with the appearance of a man who has made a very important decision and refuses to be frightened.

The winner, he was telling himself, would probably get around seven thousand dollars. That was almost exactly what the total auction money had been for the last two days, with the numbers selling for about three or four hundred each. As it was a British ship the auction would be in pounds, but he liked to do his thinking in dollars, since he was more familiar with them. Seven thousand dollars was plenty of money. Yes, it certainly was! He would ask them to pay him in hundred-dollar notes and he would take them off the ship in the inside pocket of his jacket. No problem there. He would buy a new car immediately. He would collect it on the way from the ship and drive it home just for the pleasure of seeing Ethel's face when she came out of the front door and looked at it. Wouldn't that be wonderful, to see Ethel's face when he drove up to the door in a new car? Hello, Ethel, dear, he would say. I've just bought you a little present. I saw it in the window as I went by, so I thought of you and how you always wanted one. Do you like it, dear? Do you like the colour? And then he would watch her face.

The auctioneer was standing up behind his table now. 'Ladies and gentlemen!' he shouted. 'The captain has guessed the day's run, ending midday tomorrow, at 830 kilometres. As usual, we will take the ten numbers on either side of it to make up the range. That means 820 to 840. And of course for those who think the true figure will be still further away, there will be "low field" and "high field" sold separately as well. Now, we'll draw the first number out of the hat ... here we are ... 827?'

The room became quiet. The people sat still in their chairs, all eyes watching the auctioneer. There was a certain tension in the air, and as the offers got higher, the tension grew. This wasn't a game or a joke; you could be sure of that by the way one man would look across at another who had made a higher offer – smiling perhaps, but only with the lips, while the eyes remained bright and completely cold.

Number 827 was sold for one hundred and ten pounds. The next three or four numbers were sold for about the same amount.

The ship was rolling heavily. The passengers held onto the arms of their chairs, giving all their attention to the auction.

'Low field!' the auctioneer called out. 'The next number is low field.'

Mr Botibol sat up very straight and tense. He would wait, he had decided, until the others had finished calling out their offers,

18

then he would make the last offer. He had worked out that there must be at least five hundred dollars in his account at the bank at home, probably almost six hundred. That was about two hundred pounds – over two hundred. This ticket wouldn't cost more than that.

'As you all know,' the auctioneer was saying, 'low field covers every number *below* the smallest number in the range – in this case every number below 820. So if you think the ship is going to cover less than 820 kilometres in the twenty-four hour period ending at midday tomorrow, you'd better buy this ticket. What are you offering?'

It went up to one hundred and thirty pounds. Others besides Mr Botibol seemed to have noticed that the weather was rough. One hundred and forty... fifty... There it stopped. The auctioneer waited, his hammer raised.

'Going at one hundred and fifty...'

'Sixty!' Mr Botibol called, and every face in the room turned and looked at him.

'Seventy!'

'Eighty!' Mr Botibol called.

'Ninety!'

'Two hundred!' Mr Botibol called. He wasn't stopping now – not for anyone.

There was a pause.

'Any more offers, please? Going at two hundred pounds...'

Sit still, he told himself. Sit completely still and don't look up. It's unlucky to look up. Hold your breath. No one's going to offer more if you hold your breath.

'Going for two hundred pounds...' Mr Botibol held his breath. 'Going... Going... Gone!' The man banged the hammer on the table.

Mr Botibol wrote out a cheque and handed it to the auctioneer, then he settled back in his chair to wait for the finish.

He did not want to go to bed before he knew how much money there was to win.

They added it up after the last number had been sold and it came to two thousand one hundred pounds. That was about six thousand dollars. He could buy the car and there would be some money left over too. With this pleasant thought, he went off, happy and excited, to his bed.

When Mr Botibol woke the next morning he lay quite still for several minutes with his eyes shut, listening for the sound of the wind, waiting for the roll of the ship. There was no sound of any wind and the ship was not rolling. He jumped up and looked out of the window. The sea – oh, God! – the sea was as smooth as glass, and the great ship was moving through it fast, obviously regaining the time lost during the night. Mr Botibol turned away and sat slowly down on the edge of his bed. He had no hope now. One of the higher numbers was certain to win after this.

'Oh, my God,' he said out loud. 'What shall I do?'

What, for example, would Ethel say? It was simply not possible to tell her that he had spent almost all of their two years' savings on a ticket in a ship's competition. Nor was it possible to keep the matter secret. To do that he would have to tell her to stop writing cheques. And what about the monthly payments on the television set? Already he could see the anger in the woman's eyes, the blue becoming grey and the eyes themselves narrowing, as they always did when there was anger in them.

'Oh, my God. What *shall* I do?'

It was no use pretending that he had the slightest chance now – not unless the ship started to go backwards.

It was at this moment that an idea came to him, and he jumped up from his bed, extremely excited, ran over to the window and looked out again. Well, he thought, why not? Why ever not? The sea was calm and he would have no difficulty in swimming until they picked him up. He had a feeling that someone had done something like this before, but that did not prevent him from doing it again. The ship would have to stop and lower a boat, and the boat would have to go back perhaps a kilometre to get him, and then it would have to return to the ship. That would take about an hour. An hour was about forty-eight kilometres. The delay would reduce the day's run by about forty-eight kilometres. That would do it. 'Low field' would be sure to win then – just so long as he made certain that someone saw him falling over the side; but that would be simple to arrange. And he had better wear light clothes, some-thing easy to swim in. Sports clothes, that was it. He would dress as if he were going to play deck tennis – just a shirt and a pair of shorts and tennis shoes. What was the time? 9.15. The sooner the better, then. He would have to do it soon, because the time limit was midday.

Mr Botibol was both frightened and excited when he stepped out onto the sundeck in his sports clothes. He looked around nervously. There was only one other person in sight, a woman who was old and fat. She was leaning over the rail, looking at the sea. She was wearing a heavy coat, and the collar was turned up, so Mr Botibol couldn't see her face.

He stood still, examining her carefully from a distance. Yes, he told himself, she would probably do. She would probably call for help just as quickly as anyone else. But wait one minute, take your time, William Botibol, take your time. Remember what you told yourself in your room a few minutes ago when you were changing.

The thought of jumping off a ship into the ocean hundreds of kilometres from the nearest land had made Mr Botibol – always a careful man – unusually so. He was not yet satisfied that this woman in front of him was *sure* to call for help when he made his jump. In his opinion there were two possible reasons why she might not. First, she might have bad hearing and bad eyesight. It was not very likely, but on the other hand it *might* be so, and why take a chance? All he had to do was to check it by talking to her for a moment. Second, the woman might be the owner of one of the high numbers in the competition; if so, she would have a very good financial reason for not wishing to stop the ship. Mr Botibol remembered that people had killed for far less than six thousand dollars. It was happening every day in the newspapers. So why take a chance on that either? He must check it first, and be sure of his facts. He must find out about it by a little polite conversation. Then, if the woman appeared to be a pleasant, kind human being, the thing was easy and he could jump off the ship without worrying.

Mr Botibol walked towards the woman and took up a position beside her, leaning on the rail. 'Hello,' he said pleasantly.

She turned and smiled at him, a surprisingly lovely smile, almost a beautiful smile, although the face itself was very plain. 'Hello,' she answered him.

And that, Mr Botibol told himself, answers the first question. Her hearing and eyesight are good. 'Tell me,' he said, 'what did you think of the auction last night?'

'Auction?' she asked. 'Auction? What auction?'

'You know, that silly thing they have after dinner. They sell numbers that might be equal to the ship's daily run. I just wondered what you thought about it.'

She shook her head, and again she smiled, a sweet and pleasant smile. 'I'm very lazy,' she said. 'I always go to bed early. I have my dinner in bed. It's so restful to have dinner in bed.'

Mr Botibol smiled back at her and began to walk away. 'I must go and get my exercise now,' he said. 'I never miss my exercise in the morning. It was nice seeing you. Very nice seeing you . . .'

He took a few more steps and the woman let him go without looking around.

Everything was now in order. The sea was calm, he was lightly dressed for swimming, there were almost certainly no man-eating fish in this part of the Atlantic, and there was this pleasant, kind old woman to call for help. It was now only a question of whether the ship would be delayed for long enough to help him win. Almost certainly it would.

Mr Botibol moved slowly to a position at the rail about eighteen metres away from the woman. She wasn't looking at him now. All the better. He didn't want her to watch him as he jumped off. So long as no one was watching, he would be able to say afterwards that he had slipped and fallen by accident. He looked over the side of the ship. It was a long, long drop. He might easily hurt himself badly if he hit the water flat. He must jump straight and enter the water feet first. It seemed cold and deep and grey and it made him shake with fear just to look at it. But it was now or never. Be a man, William Botibol, be a man. All right then ... now ...

He climbed up onto the wide wooden rail and stood there balancing for three terrible seconds, then he jumped up and out as far as he could go, and at the same time he shouted '*Help!*'

'*Help! Help!*' he shouted as he fell. Then he hit the water and went under.

When the first shout for help sounded, the woman who was leaning on the rail gave a little jump of surprise. She looked around quickly and saw – sailing past her through the air – this small man dressed in white shorts and tennis shoes, shouting as he went. For a moment she looked as if she were not quite sure what she ought to do: throw a lifebelt, run away and find help, or simply turn and shout. She stepped back from the rail and swung round, and for this short moment she remained still, tense and undecided. Then almost immediately she seemed to relax, and she leaned forward far over the rail, looking at the water. Soon a small round black head appeared in the water, an arm raised above it, waving, once, twice, and a small faraway voice was heard calling something that was difficult to understand. The woman leaned still further over the rail, trying to keep the little black spot in sight, but soon, so very soon, it was such a long way away that she couldn't even be sure that it was there at all.

After a time, another woman came out on deck. This one was thin and bony and wore glasses. She saw the first woman and walked over to her.

'So *there* you are,' she said.

The fat woman turned and looked at her, but said nothing.

'I've been searching for you,' the bony one continued. 'Searching all over the ship.'

'It's very strange,' the fat woman said. 'A man jumped off the deck just now, with his clothes on.'

'Nonsense!'

'Oh, yes. He said he wanted to get some exercise, and he jumped in and didn't even take his clothes off.'

'You'd better come down now,' the bony woman said. Her mouth had suddenly become firm, her whole face sharp, and she spoke less kindly than before. 'And don't you ever go wandering about on deck alone like this again. You know you're meant to wait for me.'

'Yes, Maggie,' the fat woman answered, and again she smiled, a kind, trusting smile, and she took the hand of the other one and allowed herself to be led away across the deck.

'Such a nice man,' she said. 'He waved to me.'

Mrs Bixby and the Colonel's Coat

Mr and Mrs Bixby lived in a smallish flat somewhere in New York City. Mr Bixby was a dentist, who earned an average income. Mrs Bixby was a big, active woman with a wet mouth. Once a month, always on Friday afternoons, Mrs Bixby would get on the train at Pennsylvania Station and travel to Baltimore to visit her old aunt. She would spend the night with the aunt and return to New York City on the following day, in time to cook supper for her husband. Mr Bixby accepted this arrangement good-naturedly. He knew that Aunt Maude lived in Baltimore, and that his wife was very fond of the old lady, and certainly it would be unreasonable to refuse either of them the pleasure of a monthly meeting.

'But you mustn't ever expect me to come too,' Mr Bixby had said in the beginning.

'Of course not, darling,' Mrs Bixby had answered. 'After all, she's not *your* aunt. She's mine.'

So far, so good.

As it turned out, though, the aunt was only a convenient excuse for Mrs Bixby. The real purpose of her trips was to visit a gentleman known as the Colonel, and she spent the greater part of her time in Baltimore in his company. The Colonel was very wealthy. He lived in an attractive house on the edge of the town. He had no wife and no family, only a few loyal servants, and in Mrs Bixby's absence he amused himself by riding his horses and hunting.

Year after year, this pleasant friendship between Mrs Bixby and the Colonel continued without a problem. They met so rarely – twelve times a year is not much when you think about it – that there was little or no chance of their growing bored with one

25

another. The opposite was true: the long wait between meetings made them fonder, and each separate occasion became an exciting reunion.

Eight years went by.

It was just before Christmas, and Mrs Bixby was standing on the station in Baltimore, waiting for the train to take her back to New York. This particular visit which had just ended had been more than usually pleasant, and Mrs Bixby was feeling cheerful. But then the Colonel's company always made her feel cheerful these days. The man had a way of making her feel that she was a rather special woman. How very different from her dentist husband at home, who only succeeded in making her feel that she was a sufferer from continuous toothache, someone who lived in the waiting room, silent among the magazines.

'The Colonel asked me to give you this,' a voice beside her said. She turned and saw Wilkins, one of the Colonel's servants, a small man with grey skin. He pushed a large, flat box into her arms.

'Good heavens!' she cried. 'What a big box! What is it, Wilkins? Was there a message? Did he send me a message?'

'No message,' the servant said, and he walked away.

As soon as she was on the train, Mrs Bixby carried the box into the Ladies' Room and locked the door. How exciting this was! A Christmas present from the Colonel. She started to undo the string. 'I'll bet it's a dress,' she thought. 'It might even be two dresses. Or it might be a whole lot of beautiful underclothes. I won't look. I'll just feel around and try to guess what it is. I'll try to guess the colour as well, and exactly what it looks like. Also, how much it cost.'

She shut her eyes and slowly lifted off the lid. Then she carefully put one hand into the box. There was some paper on top; she could feel it and hear it. There was also an envelope or card of some sort. She ignored this and began feeling under the paper, her fingers reaching out delicately.

'My God!' she cried suddenly. 'It can't be true!'

She opened her eyes wide and looked at the coat. Then she seized it and lifted it out of the box. The thick fur made a wonderful noise against the paper and when she held it up and saw it hanging to its full length, it was so beautiful it took her breath away.

She had never seen mink like this before. It *was* mink, wasn't it? Yes, of course it was. But what a beautiful colour! The fur was almost pure black. At first, she thought it *was* black; but when she held it closer to the window, she saw that there was a touch of blue in it as well, a deep rich blue. But what could it have cost? She hardly dared to think. Four, five, six thousand dollars? Possibly more.

She just couldn't take her eyes off it. Nor, for that matter, could she wait to try it on. Quickly she slipped off her own plain red coat. She was breathing fast now, she couldn't help it, and her eyes were stretched very wide. But, oh God, the feel of that fur! The great black coat seemed to slide onto her almost by itself, like a second skin. It was the strangest feeling! She looked into the mirror. It was wonderful. Her whole personality had suddenly changed completely. She looked wonderful, beautiful, rich and sexy, all at the same time. And the sense of power that it gave her! In this coat she could walk into any place she wanted and people would come running around her like rabbits. The whole thing was just too wonderful for words!

Mrs Bixby picked up the envelope that was still lying in the box. She opened it and pulled out the Colonel's letter:

I once heard you saying that you were fond of mink so I got you this. I'm told it's a good one. Please accept it with my sincere good wishes as a parting present. For my own personal reasons I shall not be able to see you any more. Goodbye and good luck.

Well!

Imagine that!

Just when she was feeling so happy.

No more Colonel.

What a terrible shock.

She would miss him terribly.

Slowly, Mrs Bixby began stroking the soft black fur of the coat.

She had lost one thing but gained another.

She smiled and folded the letter, meaning to tear it up and throw it out of the window. But while she was folding it, she noticed that there was something written on the other side:

Just tell them that nice generous aunt of yours gave it to you for Christmas.

The smile on Mrs Bixby's face suddenly disappeared.

'The man must be crazy!' she cried. 'Aunt Maude doesn't have that sort of money. She couldn't possibly give me this.'

But if Aunt Maude didn't give it to her, then who did?

Oh God! In the excitement of finding the coat and trying it on, she had completely ignored this important detail.

In a few hours she would be in New York. Ten minutes after that she would be home, and her husband would be there to greet her; and even a man like Cyril, living in the dark world of tooth decay and fillings and root treatments, would start asking a few questions if his wife suddenly walked in from a weekend wearing a six-thousand-dollar mink coat.

'You know what I think,' she told herself. 'I think that Colonel has done this on purpose just to drive me crazy. He knew perfectly well that Aunt Maude didn't have enough money to buy this. He knew I wouldn't be able to keep it,' she told herself.

But the thought of parting with it now was more than Mrs Bixby could bear.

'I've *got* to have this coat!' she said out loud. 'I've got to have this coat! I've got to have this coat!'

Very well, my dear. You shall have the coat. But don't worry. Sit still and keep calm and start thinking. You're a clever girl, aren't you? You've tricked him before. The man has never been able to see much further than the end of his own instruments. So sit completely still and *think*. There's lots of time.

Two and a half hours later, Mrs Bixby stepped off the train at Pennsylvania Station and walked quickly out into the street. She was wearing her old red coat again now and was carrying the box in her arms. She signalled for a taxi.

'Driver,' she said, 'do you know of a pawnbroker that's still open around here?'

The man behind the wheel looked back at her, amused.

'There are plenty of them in this area,' he answered.

'Stop at the first one you see, then, will you please?' She got in and was driven away.

Soon the taxi stopped outside a pawnbroker's shop.

'Wait for me, please,' Mrs Bixby said to the driver, and she got out of the taxi and entered the shop.

'Yes?' the owner said from a dark place in the back of the shop.

'Oh, good evening,' Mrs Bixby said. She began to untie the string around the box. 'Isn't it silly of me? I've lost my handbag, and as this is Saturday, all the banks are closed until Monday and I've simply got to have some money for the weekend. This is quite a valuable coat, but I'm not asking much. I only want to borrow enough on it to help me until Monday.'

The man waited and said nothing. But when she pulled out the mink and allowed the beautiful thick fur to fall over the counter, he came over to look at it. He picked it up and held it out in front of him.

'If only I had a watch on me or a ring,' Mrs Bixby said, 'I'd give you that instead. But I don't have a thing with me except this coat.' She spread out her fingers for him to see.

'It looks new,' the man said, stroking the soft fur.

'Oh, yes, it is. But, as I said, I only want to borrow enough money to help me until Monday. How about fifty dollars?'

'I'll lend you fifty dollars.'

'It's worth a hundred times more than that, but I know you'll take good care of it until I return.'

The man went over to a drawer and brought out a ticket and placed it on the counter. The ticket had a row of small holes across the middle so that it could be torn in two, and both halves were exactly the same.

'Name?' he asked.

'Leave that out. And the address.'

She saw the man pause, and she saw the pen waiting over the dotted line.

'You don't *have* to put the name and address, do you?'

The man shook his head and the pen moved on down to the next line.

'It's just that I'd rather not,' Mrs Bixby said. 'It's purely personal.'

'You'd better not lose this ticket, then.'

'I won't lose it.'

'Do you realize that anyone who gets hold of this ticket can come in and claim the coat?'

'Yes, I know that.'

'What do you want me to put for a description?'

'No description either, thank you. It's not necessary. Just put the amount I'm borrowing.'

The pen paused again, waiting over the dotted line beside the word 'Description'.

'I think you ought to put a description. A description is always a help if you want to sell the ticket. You never know, you might want to sell it sometime.'

'I don't want to sell it.'

'You might have to. Lots of people do.'

'Look,' Mrs Bixby said. 'I'm not poor, if that's what you mean. I simply lost my bag. Don't you understand?'

'It's your coat,' the man said.

At this point, an unpleasant thought struck Mrs Bixby. 'Tell me something,' she said. 'If I don't have a description on my ticket, how can I be sure that you'll give me back the coat and not something else when I return?'

'It goes in the books.'

'But all I've got is a number. So actually, you could hand me any old thing you wanted, isn't that so?'

'Do you want a description or don't you?' the man asked.

'No,' she said. 'I trust you.'

The man wrote 'fifty dollars' opposite the word 'Value' on both parts of the ticket, then he tore it in half down the middle and gave one half to Mrs Bixby. Then he gave her five ten-dollar notes. 'The interest is three per cent a month,' he said.

'All right. Thank you. You'll take good care of it, won't you?'

The man said nothing.

Mrs Bixby turned and went out of the shop onto the street where the taxi was waiting. Ten minutes later, she was home.

'Darling,' she said as she bent over and kissed her husband. 'Did you miss me?'

Cyril Bixby laid down the evening newspaper and looked at the watch on his wrist. 'It's twelve and a half minutes past six,' he said. 'You're a bit late, aren't you?'

'I know. It's those terrible trains. Aunt Maude sent you her love as usual. I need a drink. What about you?'

Her husband folded his newspaper neatly and went over to the drinks' cupboard. His wife remained in the centre of the room, watching him carefully, wondering how long she ought to wait. He had his back to her now, bending forward to measure the drinks. He was putting his face right up close to the measurer and looking into it as though it were a patient's mouth.

'See what I've bought for measuring the drinks,' he said, holding up a measuring glass. 'I can get it to the nearest drop with this.'

'Darling, how clever.'

I really must try to make him change the way he dresses, she told herself. His suits are just too silly. There had been a time when she thought they were wonderful, those old-fashioned jackets and narrow trousers, but now they simply seemed silly. You had to have a special sort of face to wear things like that, and Cyril just didn't have it. It was a fact that in the office he always greeted female patients with his white coat unbuttoned so that they could see his clothes beneath; in some strange way this was clearly meant to give the idea that he was a bit of a ladies' man. But Mrs Bixby knew better. It meant nothing.

'Thank you, darling,' she said, taking the drink and seating herself in an armchair with her handbag on her knees. 'And what did *you* do last night?'

'I stayed on in the office and did some work. I got my accounts up to date.'

'Now, really, Cyril, it's time you let other people do your paperwork for you. You're much too important for that sort of thing.'

'I prefer to do everything myself.'

'I know you do, darling, and I think it's wonderful. But I don't want you to get too tired. Why doesn't that Pulteney woman do the accounts? That's part of her job, isn't it?'

'She does do them. But I have to decide on the prices first. She doesn't know who's rich and who isn't.'

'This drink is perfect,' Mrs Bixby said, setting down her glass on the side table. 'Quite perfect.' She opened her bag as if to look for something. 'Oh, look!' she cried, seeing the ticket. 'I forgot to show you this! I found it just now on the seat of my taxi. It's got a number on it, and I thought it might be worth having, so I kept it.'

She handed the small piece of stiff brown paper to her husband, who took it in his fingers and began examining it closely, as if it were a problem tooth.

'You know what this is?' he said slowly.

'No, dear, I don't.'

'It's a pawn ticket.'

'A what?'

'A ticket from a pawnbroker's. Here's the name and address of the shop.'

'Oh dear, I *am* disappointed. I was hoping it might be a ticket for a horse race or something.'

'There's no reason to be disappointed,' Cyril Bixby said. 'As a matter of fact this could be rather amusing.'

'Why could it be amusing, darling?'

He began explaining to her exactly how a pawn ticket worked and particularly that anyone possessing the ticket could claim whatever it was. She listened patiently until he had finished.

'You think it's worth claiming?' she asked.

'I think it's worth finding out what it is. You see this figure of fifty dollars that's written here? Do you know what it means?'

'No, dear, what does it mean?'

'It means that the thing in question is almost certain to be something quite valuable.'

'You mean it'll be worth fifty dollars?'

'More like five hundred.'

'Five hundred!'

'Don't you understand?' he said. 'A pawnbroker never gives you more than about a tenth of the real value.'

'Good heavens! I never knew that.'

'There's a lot of things you don't know, my dear. Now you

listen to me. As there's no name and address of the owner...'

'But surely there's something to say who it belongs to?'

'Not a thing. People often do that. They don't want anyone to know they've been to a pawnbroker. They're ashamed of it.'

'Then you think we can keep it?'

'Of course we can keep it. This is now *our* ticket.'

'You mean *my* ticket,' Mrs Bixby said firmly. 'I found it.'

'My dear girl, what *does* it matter? The important thing is that we are now in a position to go and claim it any time we like for only fifty dollars. How about that?'

'Oh, what fun!' she cried. 'I think it's very exciting, especially when we don't even know what it is. It could be *anything*, isn't that right, Cyril? Anything at all!'

'Certainly it could, although it's most likely to be either a ring or a watch.'

'But wouldn't it be wonderful if it were something really valuable?'

'We can't know what it is yet, my dear. We shall just have to wait and see.'

'I think it's wonderful! Give me the ticket and I'll rush over early on Monday morning and find out!'

'I think I'd better do that.'

'Oh no!' she cried. 'Let *me* do it!'

'I think not. I'll collect it on my way to work.'

'But it's *my* ticket! *Please* let me do it, Cyril! Why should *you* have all the fun?'

'You don't know these pawnbrokers, my dear. You could get cheated.'

'I wouldn't get cheated, honestly I wouldn't. Give the ticket to me, please.'

'Also you have to have fifty dollars,' he said, smiling. 'You have to pay out fifty dollars in cash before they'll give it to you.'

'I've got that,' she said. 'I think.'

'I'd rather you didn't handle it, if you don't mind.'

'But Cyril, I *found* it. Whatever it is, it's mine, isn't that right?'

'Of course it's yours, my dear. There's no need to get so annoyed about it.'

'I'm not. I'm just excited, that's all.'

'I suppose you haven't thought that this might be something particularly male. It isn't only women that go to pawnbrokers, you know.'

'In that case, I'll give it to you for Christmas,' Mrs Bixby said generously. 'With pleasure. But if it's a woman's thing, I want it myself. Is that agreed?'

'That sounds very fair. Why don't you come with me when I collect it?'

Mrs Bixby was about to say yes to this, but stopped herself just in time. She had no wish to be greeted like an old customer by the pawnbroker in her husband's presence.

'No,' she said slowly. 'I don't think I will. You see, it'll be even more exciting if I stay here and wait. Oh, I do hope it isn't going to be something that neither of us wants.'

'You've got a point there,' he said. 'If I don't think it's worth fifty dollars, I won't even take it.'

'But you said it would be worth five hundred.'

'I'm quite sure it will. Don't worry.'

'Oh, Cyril, I can hardly wait! Isn't it exciting?'

'It's amusing,' he said, slipping the ticket into his jacket pocket. 'There's no doubt about that.'

Monday morning came at last, and after breakfast Mrs Bixby followed her husband to the door and helped him on with his coat.

'Don't work too hard, darling,' she said. 'Home at six?'

'I hope so.'

'Are you going to have time to go to that pawnbroker?' she asked.

'My God, I forgot all about it. I'll take a taxi and go there now. It's on my way.'

'You haven't lost the ticket, have you?'

'I hope not,' he said, feeling in his jacket pocket. 'No, here it is.'

'And you have enough money?'

'Yes.'

'Darling,' she said, standing close to him and straightening his tie, which was perfectly straight. 'If it happens to be something nice, something you think I might like, will you telephone me as soon as you get to the office?'

'If you want me to, yes.'

'You know, I'm hoping it'll be something for you, Cyril. I'd much rather it was for you than for me.'

'That's very generous of you, my dear. Now I must hurry.'

About an hour later, when the telephone rang, Mrs Bixby was across the room so fast she had the receiver to her ear before the first ring had finished.

'I've got it!' he said.

'You have! Oh, Cyril, what was it? Was it something good?'

'Good!' he cried. 'It's wonderful! You wait until you see this! You'll faint!'

'Darling, what is it? Tell me quickly.'

'You're a lucky girl, that's what you are.'

'It's for me, then?'

'Of course it's for you, though I can't understand how the pawnbroker only paid fifty dollars for it. Someone's crazy.'

'Cyril! Tell me! I can't bear it!'

'You'll go crazy when you see it.'

'What is it?'

'Try to guess.'

Mrs Bixby paused. Be careful, she told herself. Be very careful now.

'A diamond ring,' she said.

'Wrong.'

'What then?'

'I'll help you. It's something you can wear.'

'Something I can wear? You mean like a hat?'

'No, it's not a hat,' he said, laughing.

'Cyril! Why don't you tell me?'

'Because I want it to be a surprise. I'll bring it home with me this evening.'

'No you won't!' she cried. 'I'm coming right down there to get it now!'

'I'd rather you didn't do that.'

'Don't be silly, darling. Why shouldn't I come?'

'Because I'm too busy. I'm half an hour behind already.'

'Then I'll come in the lunch hour. All right?'

'I'm not having a lunch hour. Oh, well, come at 1.30 then, while I'm having a sandwich. Goodbye.'

At half past one exactly, Mrs Bixby arrived at Mr Bixby's place of business and rang the bell. Her husband, in his white dentist's coat, opened the door himself.

'Oh, Cyril, I'm so excited!'

'So you should be. You're a lucky girl, did you know that?' He led her down the passage and into his room.

'Go and have your lunch, Miss Pulteney,' he said to his secretary, who was busy putting instruments away. 'You can finish that when you come back.' He waited until the girl had gone, then he walked over to a cupboard that he used for hanging up his clothes and stood in front of it, pointing with his finger. 'It's in there,' he said. 'Now – shut your eyes.'

Mrs Bixby did as she was told. Then she took a deep breath and held it, and in the silence that followed she could hear him opening the cupboard door, and there was a soft sound as he pulled something out from among the other things hanging there.

'All right! You can look!'

'I don't dare to,' she said, laughing.

'Go on. Have a look.'

She opened one eye just a little, just enough to give her a dark misty view of the man standing there in his white coat holding something up in the air.

'Mink!' he cried. 'Real mink!'

At the sound of the magic word she opened her eyes quickly, and at the same time she actually started forward in order to seize the coat in her arms.

But there was no coat. There was only a stupid little fur neckpiece hanging from her husband's hand.

'Just look at that!' he said, waving it in front of her face.

Mrs Bixby put a hand up to her mouth and started backing away. I'm going to scream, she told herself. I just know it. I'm going to scream.

'What's the matter, my dear? Don't you like it?' He stopped waving the fur and stood looking at her, waiting for her to say something.

'Why, yes,' she said slowly. 'I . . . I . . . think it's . . . it's lovely . . . really lovely.'

'It quite took your breath away for a moment, didn't it?'

'Yes, it did.'

'Very good quality,' he said. 'Fine colour too. Do you know how much this would cost in a shop? Two or three hundred dollars at least.'

'I don't doubt it.'

There were two skins, two narrow dirty-looking skins with their heads still on them and little feet hanging down. One of them had the end of the other in its mouth, biting it.

'Here,' he said. 'Try it on.' He leaned forward and hung the thing around her neck, then stepped back to admire it. 'It's perfect. It really suits you. It isn't everyone who has mink, my dear.'

'No, it isn't.'

'You'd better leave it behind when you go shopping or they'll all think we're rich and start charging us double.'

'I'll try to remember that, Cyril.'

'I'm afraid you mustn't expect anything else for Christmas. Fifty dollars was rather more than I was going to spend.'

He turned away and went over to the sink and began washing his hands. 'Go and buy yourself a nice lunch now, my dear. I'd take you out myself, but I've got old man Gorman in the waiting room. There's a problem with his false teeth.'

Mrs Bixby moved towards the door.

I'm going to kill that pawnbroker, she told herself. I'm going right back there to the shop this very minute and I'm going to throw this dirty neckpiece right in his face, and if he refuses to give me back my coat I'm going to kill him.

'Did I tell you that I was going to be late home tonight?' Cyril Bixby said, still washing his hands. 'It'll probably be at least 8.30 the way things look at the moment. It may even be nine.'

'Yes, all right. Goodbye.' Mrs Bixby went out, banging the door shut behind her.

At that moment, Miss Pulteney, the secretary, came sailing past her down the passage on her way to lunch.

'Isn't it a beautiful day?' Miss Pulteney said as she went by, flashing a smile. She was walking in a very proud and confident manner, and she looked like a queen, just exactly like a queen in the beautiful black mink coat that the Colonel had given to Mrs Bixby.

The Way up to Heaven

All her life, Mrs Foster had had such a strong fear of missing a train, a plane, a boat or even the start of a play that her fear was almost an illness. In other respects, she was not a particularly nervous woman, but just the thought of being late on occasions like these would throw her into a terrible state. As a result, a small muscle in the corner of her left eye would begin to tremble. It was not very much, but the annoying thing was that the problem refused to disappear until an hour or so after the train or plane – or whatever it was – had been safely caught.

It is really strange how in certain people a simple fear about a thing like catching a train can grow into serious anxiety. At least half an hour before it was time to leave the house for the station, Mrs Foster would step out of the lift all ready to go, and then, as she was unable to sit down, she would move about from room to room until her husband, who must have known about her state of mind, finally joined her and suggested in a cool dry voice that perhaps they had better go now, had they not?

Mr Foster may possibly have had a right to be annoyed by this silliness of his wife's, but he could have had no excuse for increasing her anxiety by keeping her waiting unnecessarily. It is not, of course, certain that this is what he did, but whenever they were going somewhere, his timing was so exact – just a minute or two late, you understand – and his manner so calm that it was hard to believe that he was not purposely causing pain to the unhappy lady. He must have known that she would never dare to call out and tell him to hurry. He had trained her too well for that. He must also have known that if he was prepared to wait just a little longer than was wise, he could make her nearly crazy. On one or two special occasions in the later years of their married life, it seemed almost as though he had *wanted* to miss the train, simply to increase the poor woman's suffering.

If the husband *was* guilty, what made his behaviour doubly unreasonable was the fact that, with the exception of this one small weakness, Mrs Foster was, and always had been, a good and loving wife. For over thirty years, she had served him loyally and well. There was no doubt about this. Even she knew it, and although she had for years refused to let herself believe that Mr Foster would ever consciously hurt her, there had been times recently when she had begun to wonder.

Mr Eugene Foster, who was nearly seventy years old, lived with his wife in a large six-floor house in New York City, on East 62nd Street, and they had four servants. It was a dark, cheerless place, and few people came to visit them. But on this particular morning in January, the house had come alive and there was a great deal of activity. One servant was leaving piles of dustsheets in every room, while another was covering the furniture with them. The butler was bringing down cases and putting them in the hall. The cook kept coming up from the kitchen to have a word with the butler, and Mrs Foster herself, in an old-fashioned fur coat and a black hat, was running from room to room and pretending to organize these operations. Actually, she was thinking of nothing at all except the fact that she was going to miss her plane if her husband didn't come out of his study soon and get ready.

'What time is it, Walker?' she asked the butler as she passed him.

'It's ten minutes past nine, madam.'

'And has the car come?'

'Yes, madam, it's waiting. I'm just going to put the luggage in now.'

'It takes an hour to get to the airport,' she said. 'My plane leaves

41

at eleven. I have to be there half an hour before that to check in. I shall be late. I just *know* I'm going to be late.'

'I think you have plenty of time, madam,' the butler said kindly. 'I warned Mr Foster that you must leave at 9.15. There's still another five minutes.'

'Yes, Walker, I know, I know. But get the luggage in quickly, will you, please?'

She began walking up and down the hall, and whenever the butler came by, she asked him the time. This, she kept telling herself, was the *one* plane she must not miss. It had taken months to persuade her husband to allow her to go. If she missed it, he might easily decide that she should forget the whole thing. And the trouble was that he was determined to go to the airport with her to say goodbye.

'Dear God,' she said out loud, 'I'm going to miss it. I know, I know, I *know* I'm going to miss it.' The little muscle beside the left eye was trembling violently now. The eyes themselves were very close to tears.

'What time is it, Walker?'

'It's eighteen minutes past, madam.'

'Now I really *will* miss it!' she cried. 'Oh, I wish he would come!'

This was an important journey for Mrs Foster. She was going all alone to Paris to visit her daughter, her only child, who was married to a Frenchman. Mrs Foster did not like the Frenchman very much, but she was fond of her daughter, and, more than that, she had developed a great desire to see her three grandchildren. She knew them only from the many photographs that she had received and that she kept putting up all over the house. They were beautiful, these children. She loved them, and each time a new picture arrived she would carry it away and sit with it for a long time, examining it lovingly and searching the small faces for signs of that old satisfying blood likeness that meant so much.

And now, recently, she had come more and more to feel that she did not really wish to end her days in a place where she could not be near these children, and let them visit her, and take them for walks, and buy them presents, and watch them grow. She knew, of course, that it was wrong and in a way disloyal to have thoughts like these while her husband was still alive. She knew also that although he was no longer active in business, he would never agree to leave New York and live in Paris. It was extremely surprising that he had ever agreed to let her fly over there alone for six weeks to visit them. But, oh, how she wished she could live there always, and be close to them!

'Walker, what time is it?'

'Twenty-two minutes past, madam.'

As he spoke, a door opened and Mr Foster came into the hall. He stood for a moment, looking carefully at his wife, and she looked back at him – at this small but neat old man with the large bearded face.

'Well,' he said, 'I suppose perhaps we'd better go soon if you want to catch that plane.'

'*Yes*, dear – *yes*! Everything's ready. The car's waiting.'

'That's good!' he said. With his head over to one side, he was watching her closely.

'Here's Walker with your coat, dear. Put it on,' she said.

'I'll be with you in a moment,' he said. 'I'm just going to wash my hands.'

She waited for him, and the tall butler stood beside her, holding the coat and the hat.

'Walker, will I miss it?'

'No, madam,' the butler answered. 'I think you'll catch it all right.'

Then Mr Foster appeared again, and the butler helped him to put on his coat. Mrs Foster hurried outside and got into the hired car. Her husband came after her, but he walked down the steps slowly, pausing halfway to look up at the sky and to smell the cold morning air.

'It looks a bit foggy,' he said as he sat down beside her. 'And it's always worse out there at the airport. I shouldn't be surprised if the flight can't take off.'

'Don't say that, dear – *please*.'

They didn't speak again until the car had crossed over the river to Long Island.

'I arranged everything with the servants,' Mr Foster said. 'They're all going away today. I gave them half-pay for six weeks and told Walker I'd write to him when we wanted them back.'

'Yes,' she said. 'He told me.'

'I'll move into the club tonight. It'll be a nice change, staying at the club.'

'Yes, dear. I'll write to you.'

'I'll call in at the house occasionally to see that everything's all right and to collect the mail.'

'But don't you really think Walker should stay there all the time to look after things?' she asked nervously.

'Nonsense. It's quite unnecessary. And I'd have to pay him full wages.'

'Oh, yes,' she said. 'Of course.'

'What's more, you never know what people do when they're left alone in a house,' Mr Foster announced, and with that he took out a cigarette and lit it with a gold lighter.

She sat still in the car, with her hands held tightly together.

'Will you write to me?' she asked.

'I'll see,' he said. 'But I doubt it. You know I don't like letter-writing unless there's something particular to say.'

'Yes, dear, I know. So don't trouble yourself.'

They drove on, and as they came nearer to the flat land on which the airport was built, the fog began to thicken and the car had to slow down.

44

'Oh, dear!' cried Mrs Foster. 'I'm *sure* I'm going to miss it now! What time is it?'

'Stop worrying,' the old man said. 'It doesn't matter. They never fly in this sort of weather. I don't know why you came out at all.'

She could not be sure, but it seemed to her that there was suddenly a new note in his voice, and she turned to look at him. It was difficult to notice any change in his expression under all that hair.

'Of course,' he went on, 'if by any chance it *does* go, then I agree with you – you'll be certain to miss it now. Why don't you get used to the idea?'

She turned away and looked through the window at the fog. It seemed to be getting thicker as they went along, and now she could only just see the edge of the road. She knew that her husband's eyes were still on her. She looked at him again, and this time a wave of terror swept over her as she noticed that his eyes were fixed on the little place in the corner of her eye where she could feel the muscle trembling.

'Won't you?' he said.

'Won't I what?'

'Be sure to miss it now if it goes? We can't drive fast in this fog.'

He didn't speak to her any more after that. The car drove slowly on and on. The driver had a yellow lamp directed onto the edge of the road, and this helped him to keep going. Other lights, some white and some yellow, kept coming out of the fog towards them, and there was an especially bright one that followed close behind them all the time.

Suddenly the driver stopped the car.

'There!' Mr Foster cried. 'We're stuck. I knew it.'

'No, sir,' the driver said, turning round. 'This is the airport.'

Without a word, Mrs Foster jumped out and hurried through the main entrance into the building. There was a crowd of people inside, mostly unhappy passengers standing around the ticket counters. She pushed her way through and spoke to the clerk.

'Yes,' he said. 'Your flight has been delayed. But please don't go away. We're expecting this weather to clear at any moment.'

She went back to her husband, who was still sitting in the car, and told him the news. 'But don't wait, dear,' she said. 'There's no sense in that.'

'I won't,' he answered, 'as long as the driver can get me back. Can you get me back, driver?'

'I think so,' the man said.

'Is the luggage out?'

'Yes, sir.'

'Goodbye, dear,' Mrs Foster said, leaning into the car and giving her husband a small kiss on the rough grey fur of his cheek.

'Goodbye,' he answered. 'Have a good trip.'

The car drove off, and Mrs Foster was left alone.

The rest of the day was like a bad dream. She sat for hour after hour on a seat as close to the airline desk as possible, and every thirty minutes or so she got up and asked the clerk if the situation had changed. She always received the same reply – that she must continue to wait, because the fog might blow away at any moment. It was not until after six in the evening that it was announced that the flight had been delayed until eleven o'clock the next morning.

Mrs Foster did not quite know what to do when she heard this news. She stayed sitting on her seat for at least another half-hour, wondering, in a tired sort of way, where she might go to spend the night. She hated to leave the airport. She didn't wish to see her husband. She was frightened that in one way or another he would, in the end, manage to prevent her from getting to France. She would have liked to remain just where she was, sitting on the seat all night. That would be the safest. But she was already very

46

tired, and it did not take her long to realize that this was a stupid thing for an old lady to do. So in the end she went to a phone and called the house.

Her husband, who was on the point of leaving for his club, answered it himself. She told him the news, and asked whether the servants were still there.

'They've all gone,' he told her.

'In that case, dear, I'll just get myself a room somewhere for the night. And don't worry yourself about it at all.'

'That would be silly,' he said. 'You've got a large house available here. Use it.'

'But, dear, it's *empty*.'

'Then I'll stay with you myself.'

'There's no food in the house. There's nothing.'

'Then eat before you come in. Don't be so stupid, woman! Everything you do, you seem to want to make a problem out of it.'

'Yes,' she said. 'I'm sorry. I'll get myself a sandwich here, and then I'll come home.'

Outside, the fog had cleared a little, but it was still a long, slow drive in the taxi, and she did not arrive back at the house on 62nd Street until fairly late.

Her husband came out of his study when he heard her coming in. 'Well,' he said, standing by the door, 'how was Paris?'

'We leave at eleven in the morning,' she answered. 'It's definite.'

'You mean, if the fog clears.'

'It's clearing now. There's a wind coming up.'

'You look tired,' he said. 'You must have had an anxious day.'

'It wasn't very comfortable. I think I'll go straight to bed.'

'I've ordered a car for the morning,' he said. 'Nine o'clock.'

'Oh, thank you, dear. And I certainly hope you're not going to go to the trouble of coming all the way out again to see me off.'

'No,' he said slowly. 'I don't think I will. But there's no reason why you shouldn't drop me at the club on your way.'

She looked at him, and at that moment he seemed to be standing a long way off from her. He was suddenly so small and far away that she couldn't be sure what he was doing, or what he was thinking, or even what he was.

'The club is in the city centre,' she said. 'It isn't on the way to the airport.'

'But you'll have plenty of time, my dear. Don't you want to drop me at the club?'

'Oh, yes – of course.'

'That's good. Then I'll see you in the morning at nine.'

She went up to her bedroom on the second floor, and she was so tired that she fell asleep soon after she lay down.

Next morning, Mrs Foster was up early, and by 8.30 she was downstairs and ready to leave.

Shortly after nine, her husband appeared. 'Did you make any coffee?' he asked.

'No, dear. I thought you'd get a nice breakfast at the club. The car is here. It's been waiting. I'm all ready to go.'

They were standing in the hall – they always seemed to be meeting in the hall these days.

'Your luggage?'

'It's at the airport.'

'Ah, yes,' he said. 'Of course. And if you're going to take me to the club first, I suppose we'd better go fairly soon, hadn't we?'

'Yes!' she cried. 'Oh, yes – *please*!'

'I'm just going to get a packet of cigarettes. I'll be with you in a moment. You get in the car.'

She turned and went out to where the driver was standing, and he opened the car door for her.

'What time is it?' she asked him.

'About 9.15.'

Mr Foster came out five minutes later, and watching him as he walked slowly down the steps, she noticed that his legs were like goat's legs in those narrow trousers that he wore. As on the day before, he paused halfway down the steps to smell the air and to examine the sky. The weather was still not quite clear, but there was a little sun forcing its way through the mist.

'Perhaps you'll be lucky this time,' he said as he settled himself beside her in the car.

'Hurry, please,' she said to the driver. 'Please start the car. I'm late.'

'*Just* a moment!' Mr Foster said suddenly. 'Wait a moment, driver, will you?'

'What is it, dear?' She saw him searching the pockets of his overcoat.

'I had a little present I wanted you to take to Ellen,' he said. 'Now, where is it? I'm sure I had it in my hand as I came down.'

'I never saw you carrying anything. What sort of present?'

'A little box wrapped up in white paper. I forgot to give it to you yesterday. I don't want to forget it today.'

'A little box!' Mrs Foster cried. 'I never saw any little box!' She began hunting feverishly in the back of the car.

Her husband continued searching through the pockets of his coat. Then he unbuttoned the coat and felt around in his jacket.

'I must have left it in my bedroom. I won't be a moment.'

'Oh, *please*!' she cried. 'We haven't got time! *Please* leave it! You can post it to her. It's only one of those silly combs in any case. You're always giving her combs.'

'And what's wrong with combs, may I ask?' he said, angry that she should have lost her temper for once.

'Nothing, dear, I'm sure. But . . .'

'Stay here!' he commanded. 'I'm going to get it.'

'Be quick, dear! Oh, *please* be quick!'

She sat still, waiting and waiting.

'Driver, what time is it?'

The man looked at his watch. 'Nearly 9.30.'

'Can we get to the airport in an hour?'

'Just about.'

At this point, Mrs Foster suddenly spotted a corner of something white down in the crack of the seat on the side where her husband had been sitting. She reached over and pulled out a small paper-wrapped box, and at the same time she couldn't help noticing that it was stuck down there very firmly and deep, as if with the help of a pushing hand.

'Here it is!' she cried. 'I've found it! Oh, dear, and now he'll be up there for ever, searching for it! Driver, quickly – run in and call him down, will you please?'

The driver did not care very much for any of this, but he got out of the car and went up the steps to the front door. Then he turned and came back. 'The door's locked,' he announced. 'Have you got a key?'

'Yes – wait a minute.' She began hunting in her bag. Her little face was tight with anxiety. 'Here it is! No – I'll go myself. It'll be quicker. I know where he'll be.'

She hurried out of the car and up the steps to the front door, slid the key into the keyhole, and was about to turn it – and then she stopped. Her head came up, and she stood there completely still. She waited – five, six, seven, eight, nine, ten seconds. From the way she was standing there, it seemed as if she were listening for a sound that she had heard a moment before from a place far away inside the house.

Yes – quite clearly she was listening. She appeared actually to be moving one of her ears closer and closer to the door. Now it was right up against the door, and for another few seconds she remained in that position, head up, ear to door, hand on key, about to enter but not entering, trying instead, or so it seemed, to hear these sounds that were coming faintly from some place deep inside the house.

Then, suddenly, she came to life again. She took the key out of the door and came running back down the steps.

'It's too late!' she cried to the driver. 'I can't wait for him, I simply can't. I'll miss my plane. Hurry now, driver, hurry! To the airport!'

The driver, if he had been watching her closely, might have noticed that her face had turned white and that her whole expression had suddenly changed. There was no longer that rather soft and silly look. A strange hardness had settled on her features. The little mouth was now tight and thin, the eyes were bright, and the voice, when she spoke, carried a new note of decision.

'Hurry, driver, hurry!'

'Isn't your husband travelling with you?' the man asked, surprised.

'Certainly not! I was only going to drop him at his club. Don't sit there talking, man. Let's go! I've got to catch a plane for Paris!'

The man drove fast all the way, and she just caught her plane. Soon she was high up over the Atlantic, sitting back comfortably in her seat, listening to the sound of the engines, flying to Paris at last. The new confidence was still with her. She felt extremely strong and, in a strange sort of way, wonderful. She was a little breathless with it all, but this was more from shock at what she had done than from anything else, and as the plane flew further and further away from New York and East 62nd Street, a great sense of calmness began to settle over her. By the time she reached Paris, she was just as strong and cool and calm as she could wish.

She met her grandchildren, and they were even more beautiful than in their photographs. Every day she took them for walks, and fed them cakes, and bought them presents, and told them stories.

Once a week, on Tuesdays, she wrote a letter to her husband –

a nice, long letter – full of news, which always ended with the words, 'Now, be sure to take your meals regularly, dear, although this is something I'm afraid you may not be doing when I'm not with you.'

When the six weeks were up, everybody was sad that she had to return to America, to her husband. Everybody, this is, except her. Surprisingly, she didn't seem to mind as much as one might have expected, and when she kissed them all goodbye, there was something in her manner and in the things she said that appeared to leave open the possibility of a return in the not too distant future.

But, like the good wife she was, she did not stay longer than planned. Exactly six weeks after she had arrived, she sent a message to her husband and caught the plane back to New York.

Arriving at New York airport, Mrs Foster was interested to find that there was no car to meet her. It is possible that she may even have been a little amused. But she was extremely calm and did not give too much money to the man who helped her into a taxi with her luggage.

New York was colder than Paris, and there were piles of dirty snow lying in the streets. The taxi stopped in front of the house on 62nd Street, and Mrs Foster persuaded the driver to carry her two large cases to the top of the steps. Then she paid him and rang the bell. She waited, but there was no answer. Just to make sure, she tried again, and she could hear the bell ringing far away in the kitchen, at the back of the house. But still no one came.

So she took out her key and opened the door herself.

The first thing she saw as she entered was a great pile of mail lying on the floor, where it had fallen after being slipped through the letterbox. The place was dark and cold. A dustsheet still covered the big clock. There was a faint and strange smell in the air that she had never smelt before.

She walked quickly across the hall and disappeared for a

moment around the corner to the left, at the back. There was something purposeful about this action. When she returned a few seconds later, there was a faint look of satisfaction on her face.

She paused in the centre of the hall, as if wondering what to do next. Then, suddenly, she turned and went across into her husband's study. On the desk she found his address book, and after hunting through it for a few minutes she picked up the phone and dialled a number.

'Hello,' she said. 'Listen – this is Number Nine, East 62nd Street . . . Yes, that's right. Could you send someone round as soon as possible, do you think? Yes, it seems to be stuck between the second and third floors. At least, I think it is . . . Right away? Oh, that's very kind of you. You see, my legs aren't too good for walking up a lot of stairs. Thank you so much. Goodbye.'

She replaced the receiver and sat there at her husband's desk, patiently waiting for the man who would be coming soon to repair the lift.

The Sound Machine

It was a warm summer evening and Klausner walked quickly through the front gate, around the side of the house and into the garden at the back. He went down the garden until he came to a wooden hut; then he unlocked the door, stepped inside and closed the door behind him.

The inside of the hut was an unpainted room. Against one wall, on the left, there was a long wooden work-surface, and on it, among a lot of wires and small sharp tools, stood a black box about three feet long.

Klausner moved across the room to the box. The top of the box was open, and he bent down and began to look inside it among the different-coloured wires and silver tubes. He picked up a piece of paper that lay beside the box, studied it carefully, put it down, looked inside the box and started running his fingers along the wires, pulling at them gently to test the connections. He looked back at the paper, then into the box, then at the paper again, checking each wire. He did this for perhaps an hour.

Then he put his hand around to the front of the box where there were three dials, and he began to turn them. At the same time, he watched the movement of the machine inside the box. As he did so, he kept speaking softly to himself. His fingers were moving quickly and carefully inside the box. His mouth was twisting into strange shapes when a thing was delicate or difficult to do, and he was saying, 'Yes . . . Yes . . . And now this one . . . Yes . . . But is this right? Is it – where's my plan? . . . Ah, yes . . . Of course . . . Yes, that's right . . .' His attention was impressive; his movements were quick; there was an urgency about the way he worked, of breathlessness, of strong controlled excitement.

Suddenly he heard footsteps on the path outside, and he

straightened and turned quickly as the door opened and a tall man came in. It was Scott. It was only Scott, the doctor.

'So this is where you hide yourself in the evenings,' the doctor said.

'Hello, Scott,' Klausner said.

'I was just passing,' the doctor told him, 'so I came to see how you are. There was no one in the house, so I came on down here. How's your throat been behaving?'

'It's all right. It's fine.'

'Now that I'm here I might as well have a look at it.'

'Please don't trouble yourself. I'm quite cured. I'm fine.'

The doctor began to feel the tension in the room. He looked at the black box on the work-surface; then he looked at the man. 'What's this?' he said. 'Making a radio?'

'No. I'm just playing around.'

'It's got rather complicated-looking insides.'

'Yes.' Klausner's mind seemed to be on something else.

'What is it?' the doctor asked. 'It's rather a frightening-looking thing, isn't it?'

'It's just an idea.'

'Yes?'

'It has to do with sound, that's all.'

'Good heavens, man! Don't you get enough of that sort of thing every day at work?'

'I like sound.'

'So it seems.' The doctor went to the door, turned and said, 'Well, I won't interrupt you. I'm glad your throat's not worrying you any more.' But he kept standing there looking at the box, anxious to know what this strange patient of his was doing. 'What's it really for?' he asked. 'You've got me interested now.'

Klausner looked down at the box, then at the doctor, and he reached up and began to rub his right ear gently. There was a pause. The doctor stood by the door, waiting, smiling.

'All right, I'll tell you.' There was another pause, and the doctor could see that Klausner was having trouble deciding how to begin.

'Well, it's like this . . . the idea is very simple really. The human ear . . . you know that it can't hear everything. There are sounds so high or so low that the ear can't hear them.'

'Yes,' said the doctor. 'Yes.'

'Well, any note which is so high that it has more than 15,000 vibrations a second can't be heard. Dogs have better ears than us. A dog could hear it. There are whistles which can only be heard by dogs.'

'Yes, I've seen one.'

'Of course you have. And up the scale, higher than the note of that whistle, there's another note. You can't hear that one either. And above that there is another and another, rising right up the scale for ever and ever and ever. There's a note that's so high that it vibrates a million times a second . . . and another a million times as high as that . . . and on and on, higher and higher, as far as numbers go, beyond the stars.'

Klausner was becoming more excited every moment. He was a small man, weak and nervous, and his hands were always moving. His large head leaned towards his left shoulder as if his neck were not quite strong enough to support it. His face was smooth and pale, almost white, and the pale grey eyes behind his steel glasses had a distant, confused look. The doctor, looking at that strange pale face and those pale grey eyes, felt that there was a quality of distance about this little person. It was as if the mind were far from where the body was.

The doctor waited for him to go on. Klausner spoke slowly. 'I believe that there is a whole world of sound around us all the time that we cannot hear. It is possible that up there in those areas where sounds are so high we can't hear them, there is a new exciting music being made, a music so powerful that it would drive us crazy if only our ears were tuned to hear it. There may be anything . . . for all we know, there may be—'

'Yes,' the doctor said. 'But it's not very likely.'

'Why not? Why not?' Klausner pointed to a fly sitting on a piece of wire on the work-surface. 'You see that fly? What sort of noise is that fly making now? None – that we can hear. But the creature may be whistling or singing a song. It's got a mouth, hasn't it? It's got a throat?'

The doctor looked at the fly and he smiled. He was still standing by the door with his hand on the door handle. 'Well,' he said. 'So you're going to check that?'

'Some time ago,' Klausner said, 'I made a simple instrument that proved to me the existence of many sounds which we cannot hear. I have often sat and watched the needle of my instrument recording the presence of sound vibrations in the air when I myself could hear nothing. And *those* are the sounds I want to listen to. I want to know where they come from and who or what is making them.'

'And is that machine on the table there going to allow you to hear those noises?'

'It may. Who knows? So far, I've had no luck. But I've made some changes in it and tonight I'm ready to try it again. This machine,' he said, touching it with his hands, 'is designed to pick up sound vibrations that are too high for the human ear, and to make it possible for us to hear them. I tune the machine in, almost like a radio.'

The doctor looked at the long, black box. 'And you're going to try tonight?'

'Yes.'

'Well, I wish you luck.' He looked at his watch. 'I must go now,' he said. 'Goodbye, and thank you for telling me. I must call again sometime and find out what happened.' The doctor went out and closed the door behind him.

For a little longer, Klausner worked on the wires in the black box; then he straightened up and in a soft excited whisper said, 'Now we'll try again . . . We'll take it out into the garden this time . . . and then perhaps . . . perhaps. Lift it up now . . . carefully . . . Oh, my God, it's heavy!' He carried the box to the door, found that he couldn't open the door without putting it down, carried it back, put it on the work-surface, opened the door, and then carried it with some difficulty into the garden. He placed the box carefully on a small wooden table that stood on the grass. He went back inside the hut and got a pair of earphones. He connected these to the machine and then put them over his ears. The movements of his hands were quick and exact. He breathed in and out through his mouth in quick, loud breaths of excitement. He kept on talking to himself with little words of comfort and encouragement, as if he were afraid – afraid that the machine might not work and afraid also of what might happen if it did.

He stood there in the garden beside the wooden table, so pale, small and thin that he looked like a sick child. The sun had gone down. There was no wind, no sound at all. From where he stood, he could see over a low fence into the next garden, and there was a woman walking down the garden with a flower-basket on her arm. He watched her for a time without thinking about her at all. Then he turned to the box on the table and pressed a button on its front. He put his left hand on the controls and his right hand on the button that moved a needle across a large central dial, like the wavelength dial of a radio. The dial was marked with many numbers, starting at 15,000 and going on up to 1,000,000.

And now he was bending forward over the machine. The needle was travelling slowly across the dial, so slowly that he could hardly see it move, and in the earphones he could hear a faint noise.

Behind this noise, he could hear the sound of the machine

itself, but that was all. As he listened, he became conscious of a strange feeling that his ears were stretching out away from his head. It felt as if each ear were connected to his head by a thin stiff wire, and that the wires were getting longer, that his ears were going up and up towards a secret and forbidden land, a dangerous world of sound where ears had never been before and had no right to be.

The needle moved slowly across the dial, and suddenly he heard a scream, a terrible scream, and he jumped and caught hold of the edge of the table. He looked quickly around him as if he expected to see the person who had screamed. There was no one in sight except the woman in the garden next door, and she had not screamed. She was bending down, cutting yellow roses and putting them into her basket.

Again it came. A throatless, inhuman scream, sharp and short, very clear and cold. The note itself had a hard metallic quality that he had never heard before. Klausner looked around him, trying to see where the noise had come from. The woman next door was the only living thing in sight. He saw her reach down, take a rose stem in the fingers of one hand and cut the stem with a pair of scissors. Again he heard the scream.

It came at the exact moment when the rose stem was cut.

At this point, the woman straightened up, put the scissors into the basket with the roses and turned to walk away.

'Mrs Saunders!' Klausner shouted, his voice high with excitement. 'Oh, Mrs Saunders!'

And looking round, the woman saw her neighbour standing in his garden. He was wearing earphones and was waving his arms and calling to her in a voice so high and loud that she became frightened.

'Cut another one! Please cut another one quickly!'

She stood still, looking at him. 'Why, Mr Klausner!' she said. 'What's the matter?'

'Please do as I ask,' he said. 'Cut just one more rose!'

Mrs Saunders had always believed her neighbour to be a rather strange person; now it seemed that he had gone completely crazy. She wondered whether she should run into the house and get her husband. No, she thought. No, he's harmless. I'll just do as he asks. 'Certainly, Mr Klausner, if you like,' she said. She took her scissors from the basket, bent down and cut another rose.

Again Klausner heard that terrible, throatless scream in the earphones; again it came at the exact moment the rose stem was cut. He took off the earphones and ran to the fence that separated the two gardens. 'All right,' he said. 'That's enough. No more. Please, no more.'

The woman stood there, a yellow rose in one hand, scissors in the other. She looked at him.

'I'm going to tell you something, Mrs Saunders,' he said, 'something that you won't believe. You have, this evening, cut a basketful of roses. You have cut through the stems of living things with sharp scissors, and each rose that you cut screamed in the most terrible way. Did you know that, Mrs Saunders?'

'No,' she said. 'I certainly didn't know that.'

'I heard them screaming. Each time you cut one, I heard the cry of pain.'

'Did you really, Mr Klausner?' She decided she would make a run for the house in about five seconds.

'You might say,' he went on, 'that a rose bush has no nervous system to feel with, no throat to cry with. You'd be right. It hasn't. But *how do you know, Mrs Saunders*' – and here he leaned far over the fence and spoke in an angry whisper – '*how do you know* that a rose bush doesn't feel as much pain when someone cuts its stem as you would feel if someone cut your wrist off with a large pair of garden scissors? *How do you know that? It's alive*, isn't it?'

'Yes, Mr Klausner. Oh, yes – and good night.' Quickly she turned and ran up the garden to her house. Klausner went back to the table. He put the earphones on and stood for a moment while listening. He could still hear the faint sound of the machine, but nothing more. He bent down and took hold of a small white flower growing up through the grass. He took it between his thumb and first finger and slowly pulled it upward and sideways until the stem broke.

From the moment that he started pulling to the moment when the stem broke, he heard a faint cry. Did the noise express pain? Or surprise? Or did it express a feeling unknown to human beings?

He stood up and took off the earphones. It was getting dark. He carefully picked up the black box, carried it into the hut and put it on the work-surface. Then he went out, locked the door and walked up to the house.

The next morning Klausner was up as soon as it was light. He dressed and went straight to the hut. He picked up the machine and carried it outside. He went past the house, out through the front gate, and across the road to the park. There he paused and looked around him; then he went on until he came to a large tree, and he placed the machine on the ground close to the trunk of the tree. Quickly he went back to the house and got an axe and carried it across the road into the park. He put the axe on the ground beside the tree. Then he looked around him again, his eyes moving nervously in every direction. There was no one about. It was six in the morning.

He put the earphones on his head and turned on the machine. He listened for a moment to its faint familiar sound; then he picked up the axe, stood with his legs wide apart and swung the axe as hard as he could at the base of the tree trunk. The blade cut deep into the wood and stuck there, and at that moment he heard the strangest noise in the earphones. It was a new noise, unlike any he had heard before – a large, noteless, low, screaming sound, not quick and short like the sound of the roses. It lasted for a minute, loudest at the moment when the axe struck, getting gradually fainter and fainter until it was gone.

Klausner looked in shock at the place where the blade of the axe had sunk into the wood of the tree; then gently he took the axe handle, worked the blade loose and threw the thing to the ground. With his fingers he touched the wound that the axe had made in the wood, touching the edges of the wound, trying to press them together to close the wound, and he kept saying, 'Tree ... oh, tree... I am sorry... I am sorry... but it will get better ... it will get better...'

For a while he stood there with his hands on the trunk of the great tree; then suddenly he turned away and hurried off out of the park, across the road, back into his house. He went to the telephone, looked in the phone book, dialled a number and waited. He held the receiver tightly in his left hand and tapped the table impatiently with his right. Then he heard a man's voice, a sleepy voice, saying: 'Hello. Yes?'

'Dr Scott?' he said.

'Yes. Speaking.'

'Dr Scott. You must come immediately – quickly, please.'

'Who is it speaking?'

'Klausner here. Do you remember what I told you last night about my experience with sound, and how I hoped I might–'

'Yes, yes, of course, but what's the matter? Are you ill?'

'No, I'm not ill, but–'

'It's half past six in the morning,' the doctor said, 'and you call me but you are not ill.'

'Please come. Come quickly. I want someone to hear it. It's driving me crazy! I can't believe it...'

The doctor heard the uncontrolled note in the man's voice. It was the same note as he was used to hearing in the voices of people who called and said, 'There's been an accident. Come quickly.' He said slowly, 'You really want me to get out of bed and come over now?'

'Yes, now. Immediately, please.'

'All right, then – I'll come.'

Klausner sat down beside the telephone and waited. He tried to remember what the scream of the tree had sounded like, but he couldn't. He could remember only that it had been loud and terrible and had made him feel sick with shock. He tried to imagine what sort of noise a human would make if he had to stand fixed to the ground while someone deliberately swung a small sharp thing at his leg so that the blade cut in deep. The same noise? No. Quite different. The noise of the tree was worse than any known human noise because of that frightening, throatless quality.

He heard the front gate being opened and he went out and saw the tall doctor coming down the path. He was carrying a little black bag in his hand.

'Well,' the doctor said. 'What's the trouble?'

'Come with me, Doctor. I want you to hear it. I called you because you're the only one I've told. It's over the road in the park. Will you come now?'

The doctor looked at him. He seemed calmer now. There was no sign of him being mentally unbalanced; he was just upset and excited.

They went across the road into the park and Klausner led the way to the great tree at the foot of which stood the long black box.

'Now please put on these earphones and listen. Listen carefully and tell me afterwards exactly what you hear. I want to be quite sure . . .'

The doctor smiled and took the earphones and put them over his ears.

Klausner bent down and turned on the machine; then he picked up the axe ready to swing. For a moment he paused.

'Can you hear anything?' he said to the doctor.

'Just a faint sound from the machine.'

Klausner stood there with the axe in his hands. He lifted it and swung it at the tree. As he swung it he thought he could feel a movement of the ground on which he stood. It felt as if the tree's roots were moving under the soil, but it was too late to stop the blow and the axe blade struck the tree and went deep into the wood. At that moment, high above them, there was a cracking sound of wood breaking and the sound of leaves brushing against other leaves and they both looked up and the doctor cried, 'Watch out! Run, man! Quickly, run!'

The doctor had pulled off the earphones and was running away fast, but Klausner stood rooted to the spot, looking up, wide-eyed, at the great branch, eighteen metres long at least, that was bending slowly downwards. It was breaking at its thickest point, where it joined the trunk of the tree. The branch came crashing down and Klausner jumped to one side just in time. It fell on the machine and broke it into pieces.

'Good heavens!' shouted the doctor as he came running back. 'I thought it had hit you!'

Klausner was looking up at the tree. His large head was leaning to one side and on his smooth, white face there was an expression of terror. Slowly he walked up to the tree and gently removed the blade from the trunk.

'Did you hear it?' he said, turning to the doctor.

The doctor was still out of breath from running and the excitement. 'Hear what?'

'In the earphones. Did you hear anything when the axe struck?'

The doctor began to rub the back of his neck. 'Well,' he said, 'I think . . .' He paused and bit his lower lip. 'No, I'm not sure. I couldn't be sure. I don't suppose I had the earphones on for more than a second after the axe struck.' He was speaking quickly, rather crossly.

'Yes, yes, but what did you hear?'

'I don't know,' the doctor said. 'I don't know what I heard. Probably the noise of the branch breaking.'

'What did it sound like? *Exactly* what did it sound like?' asked Klausner, looking hard at the doctor.

'How could I tell, with half the tree falling on me? I had to run for my life!' The doctor certainly seemed nervous. Klausner felt it now. The doctor moved his feet and half turned to go. 'Well,' he said, 'we'd better get back.'

'Look,' said the little man, and now his smooth white face became suddenly filled with colour. 'Look. Stitch this up.' He pointed to the wound that the axe had made in the tree trunk. 'Stitch this up quickly.'

'Don't be silly,' said the doctor.

'Do as I say. Stitch it up!' Klausner was holding the axe, and he spoke softly, in a strange, almost threatening way.

'Don't be silly. I can't stitch through wood. Come on. Let's get back.'

'So you can't stitch through wood?'

'No, of course not.'

'Have you got any iodine in your bag?'

'Yes.'

'Then paint the wound with iodine. It'll sting, but that can't be helped.'

'Now let's not be stupid. Let's get back to the house and then . . .'

'*Paint the cut with iodine!*'

The doctor saw Klausner's hands tightening on the axe handle. The only other thing he could do was to run away fast, and he certainly wasn't going to do that.

'All right,' he said. 'I'll paint it with iodine.'

He got his black bag, opened it and took out a bottle of iodine and some cotton wool. He went up to the tree trunk, opened the

65

bottle, poured some iodine onto the cotton wool and began to rub it into both cuts. He kept one eye on Klausner, who was standing completely still with the axe in his hands, watching him.

'There you are,' the doctor said. 'It's done.'

Klausner came closer and carefully examined the two wounds in the tree. 'You'll come and look at the tree again tomorrow, won't you?'

'Oh yes,' the doctor said. 'Of course.'

'And put some more iodine on?'

'If necessary, yes.'

'Thank you, Doctor,' Klausner said. He dropped the axe, and smiled a wild, excited smile, and the doctor quickly went over to him and took him gently by the arm and said, 'Come on, we must go now,' and suddenly they were walking away, the two of them, walking silently, rather hurriedly across the park, over the road, back to the house.

The Leg of Lamb

The room was warm and clean, the curtains were closed, the two table lamps were lit – hers and the one by the empty chair opposite. On the table behind her there were two tall glasses, some bottles and a bucket of ice. Mary Maloney was waiting for her husband to come home from work.

Now and again she looked up at the clock, but without anxiety: she simply wanted to please herself with the thought that each minute that went by made it nearer the time when he would come. There was a slow, smiling quality about her, and about everything she did. The position of her head as she bent over her sewing was strangely peaceful. Her skin had a wonderful clearness, since there were only three more months before the birth of her child. Her mouth was soft and her eyes, with their new calm look, seemed larger and darker than before.

When the clock said ten minutes to five, she began to listen, and a few moments later, at the usual time, she heard the car tyres on the drive, the car door closing, the footsteps passing the window, the key turning in the lock. She stood up and went forward to kiss him as he came in.

'Hello, darling,' she said.

'Hello,' he answered.

She took his coat and hung it in the cupboard in the hall. Then she made the drinks, a strong one for him and a weak one for herself; and soon she was back again in her chair with the sewing, and he was in the other, opposite, holding the tall glass with both his hands, and rolling it gently so that the ice knocked musically against the side.

For her, this was always a wonderful time of day. She knew he didn't want to speak much until the first drink was finished, and she was happy to sit quietly, enjoying his company after the long hours alone in the house. She loved to feel the presence of this man and the male warmth that came out of him when they were alone together. She loved him for the way he sat loosely in a chair, for the way he came in through a door, or moved slowly across the room. She loved the distant look in his eyes when they rested on her, the funny shape of his mouth, and especially the way he remained silent about his tiredness, sitting still with himself until the alcohol had taken some of it away.

'Tired, darling?'

'Yes,' he said. 'I'm tired.' And as he spoke, he did an unusual thing. He lifted his glass and emptied it in one swallow although there was still half of it left. She was not really watching him, but she knew what he had done because she heard the ice falling back against the bottom of the empty glass when he lowered his arm. He paused a moment, leaned forward in his chair, then he got up and went slowly over to get himself another drink.

'I'll get it!' she cried, jumping up.

'Sit down,' he said.

When he came back, she noticed that the new drink was a very strong one. She watched him as he began to drink.

'I think it's a shame,' she said, 'that when a policeman has as much experience as you have, they keep him walking around on his feet all day long.'

He didn't answer, so she bent her head again and went on with her sewing; but each time he lifted his drink to his lips, she heard the ice against the side of the glass.

'Darling,' she said. 'Would you like me to get you some cheese? I haven't made any supper because it's Thursday.'

'No,' he said.

'If you're too tired to eat out,' she went on, 'it's still not too late. There's plenty of meat and other things in the freezer, and you can have it here and not even move out of the chair.'

Her eyes waited for an answer, a smile, a little movement of his head, but he made no sign.

'Well,' she went on, 'I'll get you some bread and cheese first.'

'I don't want it,' he said.

She moved anxiously in her chair, her large eyes still watching his face. 'But you *must* have supper. I can easily do it here. I'd like to do it. We can have lamb. Or something else. Anything you want. Everything's in the freezer.'

'Forget it,' he said.

'But, darling, you *must* eat! I'll do it, and then you can have it or not, as you like.'

She stood up and placed her sewing on the table by the lamp.

'Sit down,' he said. 'Just for a minute, sit down.'

It wasn't until then that she began to get frightened.

'Go on,' he said. 'Sit down.'

She lowered herself back slowly into the chair, watching him all the time with those large, confused eyes. He had finished the second drink and was looking down into the glass.

'Listen,' he said. 'I've got something to tell you.'

'What is it, darling? What's the matter?'

He had become completely still, and he kept his head down so that the light from the lamp beside him fell across the upper part of his face, leaving his chin and mouth in shadow. She noticed that there was a little muscle moving near the corner of his left eye.

'This is going to be a bit of a shock to you, I'm afraid,' he said. 'But I've thought about it a good deal and I've decided that the only thing to do is to tell you immediately. I hope you won't blame me too much.'

And he told her. It didn't take long, four or five minutes at most, and she sat very still through it all, watching him in shock as he went further and further away from her with each word.

'So there it is,' he added. 'And I know it's rather a bad time to be telling you this, but there simply wasn't any other way. Of course I'll give you money and see that you're looked after. But there needn't really be any problem. I hope not, in any case. It wouldn't be very good for my job.'

Her first reaction was not to believe any of it. She thought that perhaps he hadn't even spoken, that she herself had imagined the whole thing. Perhaps, if she went on with her normal life and acted as if she had not been listening, then later, when she woke up again, she might find that none of it had ever happened.

'I'll get the supper,' she managed to whisper, and this time he didn't stop her.

When she walked across the room, she couldn't feel her feet touching the floor. She couldn't feel anything at all – except a slight sickness. She did everything without thinking. She went downstairs to the freezer, put her hand inside and took hold of the first object it met. She lifted it out, and looked at it. It was wrapped in paper, so she took off the paper and looked at it again.

A leg of lamb.

All right, then, they would have lamb for supper. She carried it upstairs, holding the thin bone-end of it with both her hands, and as she went through the living room, she saw him standing by the window with his back to her, and she stopped.

'I've already told you, haven't I?' he said, hearing her, but not turning round. 'Don't make supper for me. I'm going out.'

At that point, Mary Maloney simply walked up behind him and without any pause she swung the big frozen leg of lamb high in the air and brought it down as hard as she could on the back of his head.

She might just as well have hit him with a steel bar.

She stepped back, waiting, and the strange thing was that he remained standing there for at least four or five seconds. Then he crashed to the floor.

The violence of the crash, the noise, the small table overturning, helped to bring her out of the shock. She came out slowly, feeling cold and surprised, and she stood for a few minutes, looking at the body, still holding the piece of meat tightly with both hands.

All right, she told herself. So I've killed him.

It was strange, now, how clear her mind became all of a sudden. She began thinking very fast. As the wife of a policeman, she knew what the punishment would be. That was fine. It made no difference to her. In fact, it would be a relief. On the other hand, what about the child? What were the laws about murderers with unborn children? Did they kill them both – mother and child? Or did they wait until the tenth month? What did they do?

Mary Maloney didn't know. And she certainly wasn't prepared to take a chance.

She carried the meat into the kitchen, placed it in a roasting pan, turned the cooker on high, and put the pan inside. Then she washed her hands and ran upstairs to her bedroom. She sat down in front of the mirror, tidied her face and tried to smile. The smile looked rather strange. She tried again.

'Hello, Sam,' she said brightly, out loud.

The voice sounded strange too.

'I want some potatoes please, Sam. Yes, and perhaps a can of beans.'

That was better. Both the smile and the voice sounded better now. She practised them several times more. Then she ran downstairs, took her coat, and went out of the back door, down the garden, into the street.

It wasn't six o'clock yet and the lights were still on in the corner shop.

'Hello, Sam,' she said brightly, smiling at the man behind the counter.

'Good evening, Mrs Maloney. How are *you*?'

'I want some potatoes please, Sam. Yes, and I think a can of beans.'

The man turned and reached up behind him on the shelf for the beans.

'Patrick's decided he's tired and he doesn't want to eat out tonight,' she told him. 'We usually go out on Thursdays, you know, and now I haven't got any vegetables in the house.'

'Then how about meat, Mrs Maloney?'

'No, I've got meat, thanks – I've got a nice leg of lamb, from the freezer. I don't much like cooking it frozen, Sam, but I'm taking a chance on it this time. Do you think it'll be all right?'

'Personally,' the shopkeeper said, 'I don't believe it makes any difference. Do you want these potatoes here, Mrs Maloney?'

'Oh yes, they'll be fine. Two pounds of those, please.'

'Anything else?' The shopkeeper put his head on one side, looking at her pleasantly. 'How about afterwards? What are you going to give him afterwards?'

'Well – what would you suggest, Sam?'

The man looked quickly around his shop. 'How about a nice big piece of my cream cake? I know he likes that.'

'Perfect,' she said. 'He loves it.'

And when it was all wrapped and she had paid, she put on her brightest smile and said, 'Thank you, Sam. Good night.'

'Good night, Mrs Maloney. And thank *you*.'

And now, she told herself as she hurried back, she was returning home to her husband and he was waiting for his supper. She must cook it well and make it taste as good as possible, because the poor man was tired; and if, when she entered the house, she found anything unusual or terrible, then naturally it would be a shock and she'd be crazy with grief. Of course, she wasn't *expecting* to find anything. She was just going home with the vegetables on Thursday evening to cook supper for her husband.

That's the way, she told herself. Do everything right and natural. Keep things completely natural and there'll be no need for any acting at all. Therefore, when she entered the kitchen by the back door, she was quietly singing a little tune to herself and smiling.

'Patrick!' she called. 'How are you, darling?'

She put the package down on the table and went into the living room; and when she saw him lying there on the floor with his legs doubled up and one arm twisted back underneath his body, it really was rather a shock. All the old love for him came back to her, and she ran over to him, knelt down beside him, and began to cry hard. It was easy. No acting was necessary.

A few minutes later she got up and went to the phone. She knew the number of the police station, and when the man at the other end answered, she cried to him, 'Quick! Come quickly! Patrick's dead!'

'Who's speaking?'

'Mrs Maloney. Mrs Patrick Maloney.'

'Do you mean that Patrick Maloney's dead?'

'I think so,' she cried. 'He's lying on the floor and I think he's dead.'

'We'll be there immediately,' the man said.

The car came very quickly, and when she opened the front door, two policemen walked in. She knew them both – she knew nearly all the men at that police station – and she fell right into Jack Noonan's arms, crying uncontrollably. He put her gently into a chair, then he went over to join the other policeman, who was called O'Malley. O'Malley was kneeling by the body.

'Is he dead?' she cried.

'I'm afraid he is. What happened?'

In a few words she told her story about going to the corner shop and, on her return, finding him on the floor. While she was talking, crying and talking, Noonan discovered some dried blood on the dead man's head. He showed it to O'Malley, who got up immediately and hurried to the phone.

Soon other men began to arrive. First a doctor came, then two more policemen, one of whom she knew by name. Later, a police photographer arrived and took pictures, and a man who knew about fingerprints. There was a great deal of whispering beside the dead body, and the policemen kept asking her a lot of questions. But they always treated her kindly. She told her story again, this time right from the beginning. She said that Patrick had come in, she was sewing, and he had been too tired to go out for supper. She told them how she'd put the meat in the cooker – 'it's there now, cooking' – and how she'd slipped out to the corner shop for vegetables and how she had come back to find him lying on the floor.

'Which shop?' one of the policemen asked.

She told him, and he turned and whispered something to another policeman, who immediately went out into the street.

In fifteen minutes he was back with a page of notes, and there was more whispering, and through her crying she heard a few of the whispered phrases: '. . . acted quite normal . . . very cheerful . . . wanted to give him a good supper . . . beans . . . cream cake . . . impossible that she . . .'

After a while, the photographer and the doctor left and two other men came and took the body away. Then the fingerprint man went away. The others remained. They were extremely nice to her. Jack Noonan asked her if she would rather go somewhere else, to her sister's house perhaps.

No, she said. She didn't feel she could move even a yard at the moment. Would they mind very much if she just stayed where she was until she felt better? She didn't feel too well at the moment, she really didn't.

So they left her there while they searched the house. Occasionally, one of the men asked her another question. Sometimes Jack Noonan spoke to her gently as he passed by. Her husband, he told her, had been killed by a blow on the back of the head. The blow had been made with a heavy instrument, almost certainly a large piece of metal. They were looking for the weapon. The murderer might have taken it with him, but he might have thrown it away or hidden it somewhere in or near the house.

'It's the old story,' he said. 'Get the weapon, and you've got the murderer.'

Later, one of them came up and sat beside her. Did she know, he asked, of anything in the house that could have been used as a weapon? Would she have a look around to see if anything was missing − a very heavy tool, for example. She said that there might be some things like that in the garage.

The search went on. She knew that there were other policemen in the garden all around the house. She could hear their footsteps on the drive outside. It began to get late − it was nearly nine o'clock. The four men searching the rooms seemed to be getting tired, and a little annoyed.

'Jack,' she said, the next time Jack Noonan went by. 'Would you mind giving me a drink?'

'Of course I'll give you a drink. Some of this?'

'Yes, please. But just a small one. It might make me feel better.'

He handed her the glass.

'Why don't you have one yourself?' she said. 'You must be extremely tired. Please do. You've been very good to me.'

'Well,' he answered. 'It's not strictly allowed, but I might take just a drop to keep me awake.'

One by one, the others came in and she persuaded them to have a drink too. They stood around rather awkwardly with their drinks in their hands. They were uncomfortable in her presence and they tried to say cheering things to her. Jack Noonan wandered into the kitchen, came out quickly and said, 'Look, Mrs Maloney. Do you know that your cooker is still on, and the meat is still inside?'

'Oh,' she cried. 'So it is!'

'I'd better turn it off for you, hadn't I?'

'Will you do that, Jack? Thank you so much.'

When Jack Noonan returned the second time, she looked at him with her large, dark, tearful eyes. 'Jack,' she said.

'Yes?'

'Would you do something for me – you and the others?'

'We can try, Mrs Maloney.'

'Well,' she said. 'Here you all are, all good friends of Patrick's, and you're helping to catch the man who killed him. You must be very hungry by now because it's long past your supper time, and I know that Patrick would never forgive me if I allowed you to remain in the house without offering you something to eat. Why don't you eat up the lamb in the cooker? It'll be cooked just right by now.'

'I wouldn't dream of it,' Noonan said.

'Please,' she begged. 'Please eat it. Personally, I couldn't eat a thing. But it's all right for you. Then you can go on with your work again afterwards.'

They were clearly hungry, and in the end they were persuaded to go into the kitchen and help themselves. The woman stayed where she was and listened to them through the open door. She could hear them speaking to each other, and their voices were thick because their mouths were full of meat.

'Have some more, Charlie.'

'No. We'd better not finish it.'

'She *wants* us to finish it. She said so. She won't eat it.'

'All right, then. Give me some more.'

'That's a big bar the murderer must have used to hit poor Patrick,' one of them was saying. 'The doctor says the back of his head was broken to pieces just like from a very heavy hammer.'

'That's why the weapon should be easy to find.'

'Exactly what I say.'

'Whoever did it, he's not going to carry a weapon like that around with him longer than necessary.'

'Personally, I think the weapon is somewhere in the house.'

'It's probably right under our noses. What do you think, Jack?'

And in the other room, Mary Maloney began to laugh.

Birth and Fate

'Everything is normal,' the doctor was saying. 'Just lie back and relax.' His voice was far away in the distance and he seemed to be shouting at her. 'You have a son.'

'What?'

'You have a fine son. You understand that, don't you? A fine son. Did you hear him crying?'

'Is he all right, Doctor?'

'Of course he is all right.'

'Please let me see him.'

'You'll see him in a moment.'

'You are certain he is all right?'

'I am quite certain.'

'Is he still crying?'

'Try to rest. There is nothing to worry about.'

'Why has he stopped crying, Doctor? What has happened?'

'Don't excite yourself, please. Everything is normal.'

'I want to see him. Please let me see him.'

'Dear lady,' the doctor said, touching her hand. 'You have a fine, strong, healthy child. Don't you believe me when I tell you that?'

'What is the woman over there doing to him?'

'Your baby is being made to look pretty for you,' the doctor said. 'We are giving him a wash, that is all. You must allow us a moment for that.'

'You swear he is all right?'

'I swear it. Now lie back and relax. Close your eyes. Go on, close your eyes. That's right. That's better. Good girl . . .'

'I have prayed and prayed that he will live, Doctor.'

'Of course he will live. What are you talking about?'

'The others didn't.'

'What?'

'None of my other ones lived, Doctor.'

The doctor stood beside the bed looking down at the pale, tired face of the young woman. He had never seen her before today. She and her husband were new people in the town. The barman's wife, who had come to help, had told him that the husband worked at the local customs-house on the border, and that the two of them had arrived quite suddenly at the small hotel about three months before. The husband was always drunk, the barman's wife had said, but the young woman was gentle and religious. And she was very sad. She never smiled. In the few weeks that she had been there, the barman's wife had never once seen her smile. Also it was said that this was the husband's third marriage, that one wife had died and that the other had left him for rather unpleasant reasons. So it was said.

The doctor bent down and pulled the sheet up a little higher over the patient's chest. 'You have nothing to worry about,' he said gently. 'This is a perfectly normal baby.'

'That's exactly what they told me about the others. But I lost them all, Doctor. In the last eighteen months I have lost all three of my children, so you mustn't blame me for being anxious.'

'Three?'

'This is my fourth . . . in four years. I don't think you know what it means, Doctor, to lose them all, all three of them, slowly, separately, one by one. I can see Gustav's face now as clearly as if he were lying there beside me in the bed. Gustav was a lovely boy, Doctor. But he was always ill. It is terrible when they are always ill and there is nothing you can do to help them.'

'I know.'

The woman opened her eyes, looked up at the doctor for a few seconds, then closed them again.

'My little girl was called Ida. She died a few days before

Christmas. That is only four months ago. I just wish you could have seen Ida, Doctor.'

'You have a new one now.'

'But Ida was so beautiful.'

'Yes,' said the doctor. 'I know.'

'How can you know?' she cried.

'I am sure that she was a lovely child. But this new one is also like that.' The doctor turned away from the bed and walked over to the window and stood there looking out. It was a wet grey April afternoon, and across the street he could see large raindrops falling on the red roofs of the houses.

'Ida was two years old, Doctor . . . and she was so beautiful that I was never able to take my eyes off her from the time I dressed her in the morning until she was safe in bed again at night. I used to live in fear of something happening to that child. Gustav had gone and my little Otto had also gone and she was all I had left. Sometimes I used to get up in the night and walk quietly over to her and put my ear close to her mouth just to make sure that she was breathing.'

'Try to rest,' the doctor said, going back to the bed. 'Please try to rest.' The woman's face was white and bloodless, and there was a slight blue-grey colour around the nose and the mouth.

'When she died . . . I was already expecting another baby when that happened, Doctor. This new one was four months on its way when Ida died. "I don't want it!" I shouted after the funeral. "I won't have it! I have buried enough children!" And my husband . . . he was walking among the guests with a big glass of beer in his hand . . . he turned around quickly and said, "I have news for you, Klara, I have good news." Can you imagine that, Doctor? We have just buried our third child and he stands there with a glass of beer in his hand and tells me that he has good news. "Today I have been given a new post in Braunau," he says, "so you can start packing immediately. This will be a new start for you, Klara," he says. "It will be a new place and you can have a new doctor . . ." '

'Please don't talk any more.'

'You *are* the new doctor, aren't you, Doctor?'

'That's right.'

'And here we are in Braunau?'

'Yes.'

'I'm frightened, Doctor.'

'Try not to be frightened.'

'What chance can the fourth one have now?'

'You must stop thinking like that.'

'I can't help it. I am certain that there is something in our blood that causes our children to die in this way. There must be.'

'That is nonsense.'

'Do you know what my husband said to me when Otto was born, Doctor? He came into the room and looked into the bed where Otto was lying and he said, "Why do *all* my children have to be so small and weak?" '

'I'm sure he didn't say that.'

'He put his head right up to Otto's as if he were examining an insect and he said, "All I'm saying is, why can't they be better examples of human beings? That's all I am saying." And three days after that, Otto was dead. And then Gustav died. And then Ida died. All of them died, Doctor . . . and suddenly the whole house was empty . . .'

'Don't think about it now.'

'Is this one so very small?'

'He is a normal child.'

'But small?'

'He is a little small, perhaps. But the small ones are often a lot stronger than the big ones. Just imagine, Mrs Hitler, this time next year he'll be almost learning how to walk. Isn't that a lovely thought?'

She didn't answer this.

'And two years from now he will probably be talking all the time and driving you crazy with his questions. Have you settled on a name for him yet?'

'A name?'

'Yes.'

'I don't know. I'm not sure. I think my husband said that if it was a boy, we were going to call him Adolfus.'

'That means that he would be called Adolf.'

'Yes. My husband likes Adolf because it has a certain similarity to Alois. My husband is called Alois.'

'Excellent.'

'Oh, no!' she cried, raising her head suddenly from the bed. 'That's the same question they asked me when Otto was born! He needs a name immediately. That means he's going to die!'

'Now, now,' the doctor said, taking her gently by the shoulders. 'You are quite wrong. I promise you that you are wrong. I was simply asking a question, that is all. I love talking about names. I think Adolfus is a particularly fine name. It is one of my favourites. And look – here he comes now.'

The barman's wife, carrying the baby, came across the room towards the bed. 'Here is the little beauty!' she cried, smiling. 'Would you like to hold him? Shall I put him beside you?'

'Is he well wrapped?' the doctor asked. 'It is extremely cold in here.'

'Certainly he is well wrapped.'

The baby was tightly wrapped in a white woollen cloth and only his little pink head stuck out. The barman's wife placed him gently on the bed beside the mother. 'There you are,' she said. 'Now you can lie there and look at him as much as you like.'

'I think you will like him,' the doctor said, smiling. 'He is a fine little baby.'

'He has the most lovely hands!' the barman's wife cried. 'Such long delicate fingers!'

The mother didn't move. She didn't even turn her head to look.

'Go on!' cried the barman's wife. 'He won't bite you!'

'I am frightened to look. I don't dare to believe that I have another baby and that he is all right.'

'Don't be so stupid.'

Slowly, the mother turned her head and looked at the small peaceful face that lay beside her.

'Is this my baby?'

'Of course.'

'Oh . . . oh . . . but he is beautiful.'

The doctor turned away and went over to the table and began putting his things into his bag. The mother lay on the bed, watching the child and smiling and touching him and making little noises of pleasure. 'Hello, Adolfus,' she whispered. 'Hello, my little Adolf . . .'

'Ssshh!' said the barman's wife. 'Listen! I think your husband is coming.'

The doctor walked over to the door and opened it and looked out into the passage.

'Mr Hitler!'

'Yes.'

'Come in, please.'

A small man in a dark green uniform stepped softly into the room and looked around him.

'Let me shake your hand,' the doctor said. 'You have a son.'

The man smelled strongly of beer. 'A son?'

'Yes.'

'How is he?'

'He is fine. So is your wife.'

'Good.' The father turned and walked over to the bed where his wife was lying. 'Well, Klara,' he said, smiling. 'How did it go?' He bent down to take a look at the baby. Then he bent lower and lower until his face was very close to the baby's head. The wife lay sideways, looking up at him with a frightened look.

'He has the most wonderful pair of lungs,' the barman's wife announced. 'You should have heard him screaming just after he came into this world.'

'But my God, Klara . . .'

'What is it, dear?'

'This one is even smaller than Otto was!'

The doctor stepped forward. 'There is nothing wrong with that child,' he said.

Slowly, the husband straightened up and turned away from the bed and looked at the doctor. He seemed confused and frightened. 'It's no good lying, Doctor,' he said. 'I know what it means. It's going to be the same all over again.'

'Now you listen to me,' the doctor said.

'But do you *know* what happened to the others, Doctor?'

'You must forget about the others, Mr Hitler. Give this one a chance.'

'But so small and weak!'

'My dear sir, he has only just been born.'

'Even so . . .'

'That's enough!' the doctor said sharply.

The mother was crying now. Her body was shaking.

The doctor walked over to the husband and put a hand on his shoulder. 'Be good to her,' he whispered. 'Please. It is very important.' Then he pressed the husband's shoulder hard and began pushing him forward to the edge of the bed. At last, the husband bent down and kissed his wife lightly on the cheek.

'All right, Klara,' he said. 'Now stop crying.'

'I have prayed so hard that he will live, Alois.'

'Yes.'

'Every day for months I have gone to the church and begged on my knees that this one will be allowed to live.'

'Yes, Klara, I know.'

'Three dead children is all that I can stand, don't you realize that?'

'Of course.'

'He *must* live, Alois. He *must*, he *must* . . . Oh God, protect him now . . .'

Poison

It must have been around midnight when I drove home, and as I pulled into the driveway I turned off the lights of the car so that the beam wouldn't swing in through the window of the side bedroom and wake Harry Pope. But I needn't have worried. As I came up the drive I noticed that his light was still on, so he was awake – unless perhaps he'd fallen asleep while reading.

I parked the car and, counting each step carefully in the dark, went up the five steps to the house. Pushing through the screen doors, I turned on the light in the hall. Then I went across to the door of Harry's room, opened it quietly, and looked in.

He was lying on the bed and I could see he was awake. But he didn't move. He didn't even turn his head towards me, but I heard him say, 'Timber, Timber, come here.'

He spoke slowly, whispering each word carefully, separately, and I pushed the door right open and started to go quickly across the room.

'Stop, wait a moment, Timber.' I could hardly hear what he was saying. He seemed to be having difficulty in getting the words out.

'What's the matter, Harry?'

'Sshh!' he whispered. 'Ssshhh! Don't make a noise. Take your shoes off before you come nearer. *Please* do as I say, Timber.'

I couldn't understand what he was talking about, but I thought that if he was as ill as he sounded, I'd better try to please him. I bent down and took off my shoes and left them in the middle of the floor. Then I went over to his bed.

'Don't touch the bed! Whatever you do, don't touch the bed!' He was still speaking as if he'd been shot in the stomach, and I could see him lying there on his back with a single sheet covering three-quarters of his body. He was wearing a pair of pyjamas and he was sweating terribly. It was a hot night and I was sweating a little myself, but not like Harry. His whole face was wet. It looked like a bad fever.

'What is it, Harry?'

'A krait,' he said.

'A *krait*! Oh my God! Where did it bite you? How long ago?'

'Be quiet,' he whispered.

'Listen, Harry,' I said, and I leaned forward and touched his shoulder. 'We've got to be quick. Come on now, quickly, tell me where it bit you.' He was lying there very still and tense as though he were holding onto himself hard because of sharp pain.

'I haven't been bitten,' he whispered. 'Not yet. It's on my stomach. Lying there asleep.'

I took a quick step backwards. I couldn't help it, and I looked wide-eyed at his stomach, or rather at the sheet that covered it. There were a number of folds in the sheet and it was impossible to tell if there was anything under it.

'You don't really mean there's a krait lying on your stomach now?'

'I swear it.'

'How did it get there?' I shouldn't have asked the question because it was easy to see that he was not pretending. I should have told him to keep quiet.

'I was reading,' Harry said, and he spoke very slowly, taking each word in turn and speaking it carefully so as not to move the muscles of his stomach. 'Lying on my back reading and I felt something on my chest, behind the book. Then out of the corner of my eye I saw this little krait sliding over my pyjamas. Small, less than a foot long. Knew I mustn't move. Couldn't have moved if I'd wanted to. Lay there watching it. Thought it would go over the top of the sheet.' Harry paused and was silent for a few moments. His eyes looked down towards the place where the sheet covered his stomach, and I could see he was watching to make sure his whispering wasn't frightening the thing that lay there.

'There was a big fold in the sheet,' he said, speaking more slowly than ever now, and so softly that I had to lean close to hear him. 'See it, it's still there. It went under that. I could feel it through my pyjamas, moving on my stomach. Then it stopped moving and now it's lying there in the warmth. Probably asleep. I've been waiting for you.' He raised his eyes and looked at me.

'How long ago?'

'Hours,' he whispered. 'Hours and hours and hours. I can't keep still much longer. I've been wanting to cough.'

There was not much doubt about the truth of Harry's story. As a matter of fact, it wasn't a surprising thing for a krait to do. They wait around people's houses and they go for the warm places. The surprising thing was that Harry hadn't been bitten. The bite is quite deadly, except sometimes when you do something about it immediately; and kraits kill quite a number of people every year in Bengal, mostly in the villages.

'All right, Harry,' I said, and now I was whispering too. 'Don't move and don't talk any more unless you have to. You know it won't bite unless it's frightened. We'll fix it in no time.'

I went softly out of the room and brought a small sharp knife from the kitchen. I put it in my trouser pocket ready to use immediately in case something went wrong while we were still thinking out a plan. If Harry coughed or moved or did something to frighten the krait and got bitten, I was going to be ready to cut the bitten place and try to suck the poison out. I came back to the bedroom and Harry was still lying there very quietly, sweating all over his face. His eyes followed me as I moved across the room to his bed and I could see he was wondering what I'd been doing. I stood beside him, trying to think of the best thing to do.

'Harry,' I said, and now when I spoke I put my mouth almost on his ear so I wouldn't have to raise my voice above the softest whisper, 'I think the best thing to do is for me to pull the sheet back very, very gently. Then we could have a look first. I think I could do that without waking it.'

'Don't be so silly.' There was no expression in his voice. He spoke each word too slowly, too carefully, and too softly for that. The expression was in his eyes and around the corners of his mouth.

'Why not?'

'The light would frighten it. It's dark under there now.'

'Then how about pulling the sheet back quickly and brushing it off before it has time to strike?'

'Why don't you get a doctor?' Harry said. The way he looked at me told me I should have thought of that myself in the first place.

'A doctor. Of course. That's it, I'll get Ganderbai.'

I walked softly out into the hall, found Ganderbai's number in the book, lifted the phone and told the operator to hurry.

'Dr Ganderbai,' I said. 'This is Timber Woods.'

'Hello, Mr Woods. Aren't you in bed yet?'

'Look, could you come round now? And bring serum – for a krait bite.'

'Who's been bitten?' The question came so sharply it was like a small explosion in my ear.

'No one. No one yet. But Harry Pope's in bed and he's got one lying on his stomach – asleep under the sheet on his stomach.'

For about three seconds there was silence on the line. Then, speaking slowly and firmly, Ganderbai said, 'Tell him to keep quite still. He is not to move or talk. Do you understand?'

'Of course.'

'I'll come immediately!' He rang off, and I went back to the bedroom. Harry's eyes watched me as I walked across to his bed.

89

'Ganderbai's coming. He said you should lie still.'

'What in God's name does he think I'm doing!'

'Look, Harry, he said no talking. No talking at all. Either of us.'

'Why don't you be quiet, then?' When he said this, one side of his mouth started shaking slightly with rapid little downward movements that continued for a while after he had finished speaking. I found a cloth and very gently I wiped the sweat off his face and neck. I could feel the slight movement of the muscle – the one he used for smiling – as my fingers passed over it with the cloth.

I slipped out to the kitchen, got some ice, rolled it up in a cloth and brought it back to the bedroom and laid it across Harry's forehead.

'It'll keep you cool.'

He closed his eyes and sucked breath sharply through his teeth. 'Take it away,' he whispered. 'It'll make me cough.' His smiling-muscle began to move again.

The beam of a headlight shone through the window as Ganderbai's car swung around to the front of the house. I went out to meet him, holding the ice pack with both hands.

'How is it?' Ganderbai asked, but he didn't stop to talk; he walked on past me through the screen doors into the hall. 'Where is he? Which room?'

He put his bag down on a chair in the hall and followed me into Harry's room. He walked across the floor noiselessly, delicately, like a careful cat. Harry watched him out of the sides of his eyes. When Ganderbai reached the bed he looked down at Harry and smiled confidently, showing Harry it was a simple matter and he was not to worry but just to leave it to Dr Ganderbai. Then he turned and went back to the hall and I followed him.

'The first thing is to try to get some of the serum into him – with a needle.' He opened his bag and started to make

90

preparations. 'But I must do it very carefully. I don't want him to move.'

He had a small bottle in his left hand and he stuck the needle through the rubber top and began drawing a pale yellow liquid out of the bottle. Then he handed the needle to me.

'Hold that until I ask for it.'

He picked up the bag and together we returned to the room. Harry's eyes were bright now and wide open. Ganderbai bent over Harry and very carefully rolled up one arm of the pyjama top. I noticed he stood well away from the bed.

He whispered, 'I'm going to give you some serum. You'll feel the needle, but try not to move. Don't tighten your stomach muscles. Let them go loose.'

Harry looked at the needle.

Ganderbai cleaned a small area of the arm with alcohol, took the needle from my hand, and held it up to the light to check the quantity. I stood beside him, watching. Harry was watching too and sweating all over his face. Ganderbai held the needle almost flat against Harry's arm, sliding it in sideways through the skin slowly but firmly – as smoothly as into cheese. Harry looked at the ceiling and closed his eyes and opened them again, but he didn't move.

When it was finished Ganderbai leaned forward, putting his mouth close to Harry's ear. 'Now you'll be all right even if you *are* bitten. But don't move. Please don't move. I'll be back in a moment.'

He picked up his bag and went out to the hall and I followed.

'Is he safe now?' I asked.

'No.'

'How safe is he? It must give him some protection, mustn't it?' I asked.

He turned away and walked to the screen doors. I thought he was going through them, but he stopped this side of the doors

91

and stood looking out into the night.

'Isn't the serum very good?' I asked.

'Unfortunately not,' he answered, without turning round. 'It might save him. It might not. I am trying to think of something else to do.'

'Shall we pull the sheet back quickly and brush it off before it has time to strike?'

'Never! We have no right to take a risk.' He spoke sharply and his voice was a little higher than usual.

'We can't leave him lying there,' I said. 'He's getting nervous.'

'Please, please!' he said, turning round, holding both hands up in the air. 'Not so fast, please.' He wiped his forehead and stood there, thinking.

'You see,' he said at last, 'there is a way to do this. You know what we must do – we must give an anaesthetic to the creature where it lies.'

It was an excellent idea.

'It is not safe,' he continued, 'because a snake is cold-blooded and an anaesthetic does not work so well or so quickly with such animals, but it is the best thing to do. We could use chloroform . . .' He was speaking slowly and trying to think about it all while he talked. 'Now quickly!' He took my arm. 'Drive to my house! By the time you get there I shall have spoken to my boy on the telephone, and he will show you my poisons' cupboard. Here is the key of the cupboard. Take a bottle of chloroform. The name is printed on it. I'll stay here in case anything happens. Be quick now, hurry! No, no, you don't need your shoes!'

I drove fast, and in about fifteen minutes I was back with the bottle of chloroform. Ganderbai came out of Harry's room and met me in the hall. 'Have you got it?' he said. 'Good, good. I've just been telling him what we are going to do. But now we must hurry. It is not easy for him in there like that all this time. I am afraid he might move.'

He went back to the bedroom and I followed, carrying the bottle carefully with both hands. Harry was lying on the bed in exactly the same position as before with the sweat pouring down his cheeks. His face was white and wet. He turned his eyes towards me and I smiled at him confidently. Ganderbai was kneeling by the bed, and on the floor beside him was a hollow rubber tube. He began to pull a little piece of the sheet out from under the bed. He was working directly in line with Harry's stomach, and I watched his fingers as they pulled gently at the edge of the sheet. He worked so slowly it was almost impossible to see any movement, either in his fingers or in the sheet that was being pulled.

Finally, he succeeded in making an opening under the sheet and he took the rubber tube and put one end of it in the opening so that it would slide under the sheet towards Harry's body. I do not know how long it took him to slide that tube in. It may have been twenty minutes, it may have been forty. I never once saw the tube move. Ganderbai himself was sweating now, but his hands were steady. I noticed that his eyes were watching, not the tube in his hands, but the area of folded sheet above Harry's stomach.

Without looking up, he held out a hand to me for the chloroform. I put the bottle right into his hand, not letting go until I was sure that he had a good hold on it. Then he signalled with his head for me to come closer and he whispered, 'Tell him I'm going to pour it all over the bed and that it will be very cold under his body. He must be ready for that and he must not move. Tell him now.'

I bent over Harry and passed on the message.

'Why doesn't he just do it?' Harry said.

'He's going to now, Harry. But it'll feel very cold, so be ready for it.'

'Oh, God, hurry up, hurry up!' For the first time he raised his voice, and Ganderbai looked up sharply, watched him for a few seconds, then went back to his business.

Ganderbai poured a few drops of chloroform into the tube and waited. Then he poured some more. Then he waited again, and the heavy sickly smell of chloroform spread out all over the room bringing with it faint unpleasant memories of white-coated nurses and white doctors standing in a white room around a long white table. Ganderbai was pouring steadily now. He paused, held the bottle up to the light, poured some more and handed the bottle back to me. Slowly, he drew out the rubber tube from under the sheet; then he stood up. His voice was small and tired, 'We'll give it fifteen minutes. Just to be safe.'

I leaned over to tell Harry. 'We're going to give it fifteen minutes, just to be safe. But it's probably asleep already.'

'Then why don't you look and see!' Again he spoke loudly and Ganderbai jumped, his small brown face suddenly very angry. He had almost pure black eyes and he looked sharply at Harry. Harry's smiling-muscle began to move. I took a cloth and wiped his wet face, trying to stroke his forehead a little for comfort as I did so.

Then we stood and waited beside the bed, Ganderbai watching Harry all the time with a strange expression on his face. The little Indian was using all his willpower to keep Harry quiet. He never once took his eyes from the patient, and although he made no sound, he seemed somehow to be shouting at him all the time, saying: 'Now listen, you must listen, you're not going to spoil this now, do you hear me?' And Harry lay there moving his mouth, sweating, closing his eyes, opening them, looking at me, at the sheet, at the ceiling, at me again, but never at Ganderbai. But somehow Ganderbai was holding him. The smell of chloroform was terrible and it made me feel sick, but I couldn't leave the room now.

Ganderbai finally turned and signalled that he was ready to go on. 'You go over to one side of the bed,' he said. 'We will each take one side of the sheet and pull it back together, but very slowly, please, and very quietly.'

'Keep still now, Harry,' I said and I went around to the other side of the bed and took hold of the sheet. Ganderbai stood opposite me, and together we began to pull back the sheet, lifting it up and away from Harry's body, taking it back very slowly; both of us were standing well away but at the same time bending forward, trying to see under it. The smell of chloroform was horrible. I remember trying to hold my breath and when I couldn't do that any longer I tried to take small breaths so that the gas wouldn't get into my lungs.

The whole of Harry's chest could be seen now, or rather the pyjama top which covered it, and then I saw the top of his pyjama trousers. There was nothing on his stomach.

We pulled the sheet back faster then, and when we had uncovered his legs and feet we let the sheet drop over the end of the bed onto the floor.

'Don't move,' Ganderbai said, 'don't move, Mr Pope'; and he began to look around along the side of Harry's body and under his legs. 'We must be careful. It may be anywhere. It could be up the leg of your pyjamas.'

When Ganderbai said this, Harry quickly raised his head from the bed and looked down at his legs. It was the first time he had moved. Then suddenly, he jumped up, stood on his bed and shook his legs one after the other violently in the air. At that moment we both thought he had been bitten and Ganderbai was already reaching down into his bag when Harry stopped jumping around and stood still, looked at the bed he was standing on and shouted, 'It's not there!'

Ganderbai straightened up and for a moment he too looked at the bed; then he looked up at Harry. Harry was all right. He hadn't been bitten and now he wasn't going to get bitten and he wasn't going to be killed and everything was fine. But that didn't seem to make anyone feel any better.

'Mr Pope, you are of course *quite* sure you saw it in the first place?'

Harry stood on his bed in his pyjamas, looking angrily at Ganderbai, and the colour began to spread out all over his cheeks.

'Are you telling me I'm a liar?' he shouted.

Ganderbai remained completely still, watching Harry. Harry took a step forward on the bed and there was a shining look in his eyes.

'Why, you dirty little rat!'

'Be quiet, Harry!' I said.

'You dirty—'

'Harry!' I called. 'Be quiet, Harry!' The things he was saying were terrible.

Ganderbai went out of the room as if neither of us was there, and I followed him and put my arm around his shoulder as he walked across the hall.

'Don't listen to Harry,' I said. 'This thing's made him so upset that he doesn't know what he's saying.'

We went down the steps and across to where his car was parked. He opened the door and got in.

'You did a wonderful job,' I said. 'Thank you very much for coming.'

'All he needs is a good holiday,' he said quietly, without looking at me. Then he started the engine and drove off.

ACTIVITIES

'Taste'

Before you read

1 Read the Introduction to the book. Which of the following words can be used to describe Roald Dahl's stories?

   strange   charming   unusual   funny   sad   surprising

2 Look at the Word List at the back of the book, and then discuss these questions.

   a Is betting legal in your country? Make a list of activities that people make bets on. Can betting ever be dangerous, do you think?

   b France is famous for its wines, which are produced in different areas of the country. Is wine produced in your country? What kinds of food and drink are different parts of your country famous for?

   c What is the difference between a greedy person and an epicure? Do you admire epicures? Why (not)?

While you read

3 Are these sentences true (T) or false (F)?

   a The Schofields prepare the meal very carefully.   .....

   b Richard Pratt praises the Mosel wine.   .....

   c Richard has helped Mike choose the wines.   .....

   d Both men are sure they will win the bet.   .....

   e Richard tells Mike the correct name of the claret.   .....

   f Mike Schofield admires Richard's knowledge.   .....

After you read

4 Answer the following questions.

   a The writer says there is 'something evil' about Richard Pratt. Do you agree? Give your reasons.

   b Why do you think Louise finally agrees to the bet?

   c There are four women in the room. Only one understands what is happening. Who is it? How does she know?

d What do you think Mike and Richard say to each other after the end of the story? Act out their conversation with another student.

'A Swim'

Before you read

5 This story is set on a passenger ship. Discuss these questions.
  a Which words from the Word List do you think will be used?
  b What problems might there be on the ship?
  c What kinds of entertainment would you expect passengers to be offered?

While you read

6 Write the questions that have the following answers.

  a ....
  Rough, then calm, and now rough again.

  b ....
  He guesses how far the ship will travel.

  c ....
  Half way through the evening meal on the third day.

  d ....
  Close to the auctioneer's table.

  e ....
  About $7,000.

  f ....
  A car.

  g ....
  That the sea is as smooth as glass.

  h ....
  To delay the ship.

  i ....
  So that his low field number will win the auction.

  j ....
  He is going to drown.

After you read

7 Discuss these questions.

    a What mistake does Mr Botibol make about the fat woman?

    b What does she do?

    c Is there any way that the truth will ever be known? Why (not)?

'Mrs Bixby and the Colonel's Coat'

Before you read

8 Discuss these questions.

    a What kind of people is a Colonel in charge of?

    b Why do many people refuse to wear animal fur? Do people wear clothes made of fur in your country? Would you?

    c Are there pawnbrokers in your country? What kind of people make use of them? Are they a good idea or not?

While you read

9 Who is speaking? Who to?

    a 'She's not *your* aunt. She's mine.'

        .... to ....

    b 'No message.'

        .... to ....

    c 'I've *got* to have this coat!'

        .... to ....

    d 'You'd better not lose this ticket.'

        .... to ....

    e 'This could be rather amusing.'

        .... to ....

    f 'Isn't it a beautiful day?'

        .... to ....

After you read

10 Which of these sentences is true?

    a The Colonel is married to Mrs Bixby's aunt.

    b Mr Bixby never goes to Baltimore with his wife.

    c The Colonel's gift is a disappointment to Mrs Bixby.

    d Mr Bixby helped his wife get her coat back.

11 Discuss these questions.

    a At what stage in the story do you suspect that Mr Bixby knows the truth about his wife's visits to Baltimore?

    b How has Mr Bixby been deceiving his wife?

    c Do you feel sorry for either of them? Give your reasons.

'The Way up to Heaven'

Before you read

12 Discuss these questions.

    a Think about the title of this story. What do you think the story might be about?

    b The people in this story have a butler. What does this tell us about them?

    c One of the characters in this story is always worried about being late. Are you like that, or not? Is it bad manners for people to be late in your country or doesn't it matter?

While you read

13 List four things about the Fosters which make it clear that they are rich.

    ....

    ....

14 List the six ways in which Mr Foster delays his wife on her two journeys to the airport.

    a ....

    b ....

    c ....

    d ....

    e ....

    f ....

After you read

15 Answer these questions.

    a What does Mrs Foster hear as she stands outside the front door?

    b What has happened?

    c What does she decide to do?

16 Do these adjectives describe Mr Foster or Mrs Foster? Explain why.

annoying anxious calm clever cruel desperate kind
lonely nasty nervous

17 Discuss these questions.

   a Were you surprised by Mrs Foster's action?

   b Do you blame her for what she did?

   c Can you explain the title of this story now?

'The Sound Machine'

Before you read

18 There are some sounds that humans cannot hear, but that can be heard. How do we know?

While you read

19 Number these sentences in the right order, 1–12.

   a The doctor begins to feel tension in the room.   .....

   b Klausner starts the machine.   .....

   c Klausner has a visit from his doctor.   .....

   d Klausner is almost killed by the tree.   .....

   e Klausner calls the doctor as a witness.   .....

   f Klausner goes into his hut.   .....

   g Klausner hears a tree scream.   .....

   h The doctor leaves the hut.   .....

   i Klausner explains his invention.   .....

   j Klausner makes the doctor treat the tree.   .....

   k Klausner returns home.   .....

   l Klausner frightens his neighbour.   .....

After you read

20 Explain:

   a What happens in the garden

      1) What does Klausner hear?

      2) What does he think is making the noise?

      3) Does his neighbour agree?

4) What does she think?

5) How does Klausner test his idea?

b What happens in the park

1) What does Klausner hear?

2) What does he think is making the noise?

3) What does the doctor hear?

4) What does the doctor think?

21 Discuss these questions.

a What do you think Klausner will do now?

b If you heard this story from Klausner himself, what would you say to him?

c What would you do if you were the doctor?

'The Leg of Lamb'

Before you read

22 Discuss these questions.

a How many ways can you think of to cook lamb?

b How are murderers punished in your country? Do you agree with this method of punishment?

While you read

23 Complete the story. Write one word in each space.

Just before **(a)** .... o'clock one evening, Mary Maloney's **(b)** .... arrives home. After a couple of **(c)** ...., he shocks her with the news that he is going to **(d)** .... her and her unborn child. She goes into the kitchen and takes a leg of **(e)** .... from the **(f)** .... Then she **(g)** .... him with it. Mary doesn't want to **(h)** .... for her crime, so she puts the lamb in the **(i)** ...., buys **(j)** .... and **(k)** .... from the shop and returns home. She then phones the **(l)** .... and shows them her husband's **(m)** .... The policemen ask questions and then, at Mary's invitation, they **(n)** .... the lamb.

24 Discuss these questions.

    a Do you think the murderer will ever be caught now?

    b If Mary ever tells the truth, what will her defence be?

    c How sympathetic do you feel towards Mary?

'Birth and Fate'

Before you read

25 Discuss these questions.

    a The woman in this story has just given birth to her fourth child. How do you think she is feeling at the moment?

    b Do you believe in fate? If you believe in God, can you also believe in fate?

While you read

26 Find the correct endings to these sentences, below, and write the correct numbers.

    a The woman is anxious about her baby, because …   .....

    b She is her husband's third wife, because …   .....

    c She was particularly upset when Ida died, because …   .....

    d At the funeral, her husband expected her to be pleased, because …   .....

    e The baby will be called Adolfus – or Adolf, for short – because …   .....

    f Mr Hitler is worried, because …   .....

    1) they would be moving to a new town.

    2) one died and the other left him.

    3) she has already lost her other children.

    4) his father has a similar name.

    5) her two boys had already died.

    6) this baby is even smaller than his dead brother was.

After you read

27 Discuss these questions.

    a How do we know that this baby will, in fact, live?

    b What do we know about Klara and Alois? Do you think they will be good parents?

c Klara prays to God that her baby will live. How would history have been different if he hadn't lived?

'Poison'

Before you read

28 Discuss these questions.

a This story, which takes place in India, is about a small poisonous snake called a krait. A krait's bite can cause death. Are there any poisonous creatures in your country? How do people deal with them?

b Two of the characters in this story are Englishmen living in India. Why do you think they are there?

c Are there many people of different nationalities living in your country? Do they mix well, or suffer from any racism? What might cause problems between foreigners, or new citizens, and natives of your country?

While you read

29 Circle the correct answer.

a When Timber arrives home, Harry is *awake/asleep*.

b Harry says that a krait *has bitten him/is lying on him*.

c The krait is *a small one/a big one*.

d Harry tells Timber to *pull the sheet back/get a doctor*.

e The doctor gives serum to *Harry/the krait*.

f He uses chloroform on *Harry/the krait*.

g When the sheet is removed *the krait/no krait* can be seen.

h *Harry/Timber* is very grateful to the doctor.

After you read

30 Think about the title of this story. It can refer to the krait's poison, but what else could it refer to?

Writing

31 Imagine that the servant in 'Taste' said nothing and that Richard Pratt won the bet. He has married Louise Schofield. Write a letter from Louise to a close friend describing her marriage and her husband's behaviour.

32 You are the captain of the ship on which Mr William Botibol was a passenger in the story 'A Swim'. Write a report explaining what you have found out about this missing person and what you think happened.

33 Imagine that you are Miss Pulteney in the story 'Mrs Bixby and the Colonel's Coat'. You have lunch with a friend who admires your mink coat. Tell her why your dear friend Mr Bixby gave it to you, explaining how well you know him. Write your side of the conversation.

34 You are Mrs Foster in the story 'The Way up to Heaven'. Write a letter to your daughter in Paris telling her what has happened to her father, and of your plans to leave New York and live in Paris.

35 Imagine that Dr Scott has to write a report for a mental hospital about Klausner, in the story 'The Sound Machine', after he goes mad. Write this report, explaining what has happened.

36 Imagine that you are Mary Maloney from the story 'The Leg of Lamb'. You are now feeling guilty. Write a statement for the police admitting everything and explaining how and why you murdered your husband.

37 Imagine that Klara Hitler, in the story 'Birth and Fate', lives long enough to see her son Adolf become the leader of his country. Before she dies, she writes down what she feels about her son. Write her views.

38 Write the story 'Poison' from the point of view of the Indian Doctor Ganderbai.

39 Many of Dahl's stories have a surprising 'twist'. Choose two stories and say where you think the twist comes. Then show how it changes the story.

40 Choose the story you like best and explain why you like it.

WORD LIST

anaesthetic (n) a drug that stops you feeling pain

anxiety (n) the feeling of being very worried about something

approval (n) the belief that someone or something is acceptable

auction (n) a sale at which things are sold to the people who offer the most money for them; the person in charge of an *auction* is the **auctioneer**

axe (n) a tool with a wooden handle and a metal blade, used for cutting wood

butler (n) the most important male servant in a big house

chloroform (n) a liquid that makes you unconscious if you breathe it

claret (n) red wine from the Bordeaux area of France

colonel (n) someone with a high position in the army

deck (n) the flat top part of a ship that you can walk on

delicate (adj) easily becomes ill or damaged; very careful

determined (adj) with a strong desire to do something, even when it is difficult

dial (n/v) the part of a piece of equipment that you turn; the round part of a machine that shows you measurements

epicure (n) someone who enjoys good food and drink

fate (n) a power that is believed to control what happens in people's lives; the things, usually bad or serious, that happen to someone

graceful (adj) smooth and attractive

iodine (n) a dark blue chemical that is used on wounds to prevent infection

joint (n) a large piece of meat, containing a bone

krait (n) a kind of snake, found in India and South-East Asia

lungs (n pl) the two parts of your body, inside your chest, that you use for breathing

mink (n) the soft, valuable fur from a small, brown animal, use to make coats and hats

pawnbroker (n) someone who lends money in exchange for valuable objects, and can sell the objects if the money isn't repaid